ALSO BY SUSIE BRIGHT:

Sexwise

Susie Bright's Sexual Reality

Susie Sexpert's Lesbian Sex World

Editor, *Best American Erotica 1993*

and *Best American Erotica 1994*

Editor, *Herotica, Herotica 2,* and *Herotica 3*

THE BEST AMERICAN EROTICA 1995

Edited by

Susie Bright

A TOUCHSTONE BOOK
PUBLISHED BY SIMON & SCHUSTER
New York London Toronto Sydney Tokyo Singapore

TOUCHSTONE
Rockefeller Center
1230 Avenue of the Americas
New York, NY 10020

This book is a work of fiction. Names, characters,
places, and incidents either are products of the
author's imagination or are used fictitiously. Any
resemblance to actual events or locales or persons,
living or dead, is entirely coincidental.

TOUCHSTONE and colophon are registered trademarks
of Simon & Schuster Inc.

Designed by Irving Perkins Associates

Manufactured in the United States of America

10 9   8   7   6   5   4   3   2   1

Library of Congress Cataloging-in-Publication Data is
available.

ISBN 0-684-80163-9

CONTENTS

Contents

ACKNOWLEDGMENTS

This anthology of erotic writing could not have been researched and collected without the patience, enthusiasm, and discriminating appreciation of my Reading Assistant, Jon Bailiff.

Bethany Clement, my Editorial Assistant (and the only copy editor in the world who carries a red pencil in her purse "just in case") was relentlessly diplomatic and efficient from day one of our task until the very end. Thanks also to my father, Bill Bright, for proofreading and higher editorial wisdom.

Thank you to my managers Jo-Lynne Worley and Joani Shoemaker for all your guidance and support.

This 1995 volume of *Best American Erotica* is dedicated to Barbara Winslow on the occasion of her fiftieth birthday.

INTRODUCTION

I can tell you the exact moment when a rose is no longer a rose. The petals can be any shade from fire to ice, the thorns thick enough to bleed leather; that's not what makes the difference.

A rose is a rose is a rose, right up 'til the bloom you breathe parachutes into your belly, parts your legs, and pushes you right over a wet stained edge. Then the rose is no longer a rose—it's pornography.

I'm only describing the status quo; I never said it was fair. In fact, I think this dirty trick ranks right up there with the most insane injustice. Why do we appreciate and respect literature, theater, art, music—unless it arouses us? Our public passion for culture seems to have no limits, until it makes us come in our pants, and then the line is drawn: Art cannot be explicitly sexual, or it loses its claim to the throne.

One of the contributors to this year's collection of outstanding erotic fiction is a well-known writer, and in his "pre-erotic" writing days he was known as an upstanding young author, top drawer. But this year, Nicholson Baker was awarded by no less than three publications the distinction of fathering the "Worst Book of the Year," *The Fermata*. I have excerpted one of *Fermata's* scenes in this edition.

Now, did Baker get this Grandly Awful honor because he lost his grammatical marbles? Has he truly forgotten how to turn a phrase? Or is it that he has evolved
into such a bore that he can't be trusted to tell a decent
story anymore? I'm afraid that's not the case. The people who dubbed him "worst of the year" undoubtedly
read the entire *Fermata*, and if they cheated it was only
to speed ahead to the most provocative parts.

No, the reason that a famous author is taking such a
public spanking is because he willingly, in a thoroughly
premeditated fashion, wrote about fucking. And looking. And every open and willing part of the body, not to
mention a few mechanical pleasure devices.

The only reason all the rest of the authors in this book
haven't been scalded by the national literary police is
because they are not big names. They have perhaps
written even "worse" stories, if "worseness" is now
code for sexual outrage. They often write for less high-
profile publications that are reflexively protective or
censored. There are dozens of small journals and magazines that are delighted or even devoted to printing
their work. But when they do, it is a foregone conclu-
sion that the work cannot be sold in "respectable bookstores, chain bookstores, small town bookstores,
country bookstores, Southern bookstores, Midwestern
bookstores, suburban bookstores."

That's an accurate list that was quoted to me by a
magazine distributor years ago when I was editing *On
Our Backs,* my own small erotic magazine. My expert
added, "You can just forget Florida." He was referring
to the Orange Sunshine state, which is so sexually re-
pressed/obsessed in their public policy that you can't
deal in cutting-edge sexual material there without sub-

sequent prosecution. And they aren't the only ones.

Literature critics often dispense these good-girl-art/bad-girl-art distinctions as if the divide were invented by a higher aesthetic power. But it's puritanical religious mores that form the critics' choices, not enlightened opinions.

Will Blythe represented the tradition well in an *Esquire* review of *Best American Erotica 1994* when he said, "If it's good art, it isn't good porn." This parochial school of critical thought holds that good smut—because of its orgasmic result—cannot excel at prose. There's the whole mind/body split, a perfect aerial view.

It's certainly true that our shame and disgust with sexual expression has resulted in a retarded erotic genre. Imagine if we couldn't publish any recipes that incited hunger, or print any mysteries that contained unbearable suspense. We would be a nation of people with no public taste and no thrilling curiosity. As it is, we're almost there: Our erotic taste and imaginations have been stifled and ridiculed beyond belief.

Authors who have deliberately crossed the sex line and earned scholarly recognition are rare flowers. Homage to the dead: Miller, Lawrence, DeSade, a tip of the hat. They get the grudging respect that, yes, they could *write*. But the other side of the literary coin isn't pointed out: They also got a lot of people off. Don't think for a moment that their prose was not EFFECTIVE.

When an author embraces explicit sex and feeling along with the other graces—humor, tragedy, the sense of the times, the politics of boy/girl/girl/boy/boy—we should be handing out genius awards, or at least gasping, "S/he told the truth." What divine innocence. How did such writers keep their natural feelings on the page, how did they not self-censor, or corrupt and deny the muse? They thought with their dicks! And what a discipline it turned out to be.

I think the *Best American Erotica* writers knew perfectly well that you can't please everyone. Even stroke books in adult bookshops advertise themselves with titles to keep the lesbian lovers on one row and the back-door enthusiasts on another.

But one feature of new erotic writing in the 1990s is that writers are telling an intimate, true story, and if it's not perfectly autobiographical, it's one hell of a metaphor. It's not trying to convert you, it's a message in a bottle.

Contemporary erotica is about "being real," about the triumph of authenticity over commerciality. Sometimes, as in Lisa Palac's "Low-Cut," the commercial situation—a personal sex ad in the newspaper—is ironically underlined with What Really Happens when you meet the people in the ad. Even more cruelly in "Dating for Dollars," Scarlett Fever relates the sexual thrill as the exact process of a professional sting operation.

It requires supernatural powers to tell the truth about sex at the end of the century, and perhaps that is one clue to the popularity of gothic erotic literature, or even horror-erotica. *The Fermata* turns on one man's unearthly voyeuristic powers, and in Jay Michaelson's "This Spirit That Denies," it is a tortured werewolf who tells the tale. In "Cinnamon Roses," Renee Charles's truth teller is a vampire hairdresser. Robert Olen Butler's "Boy Born with Tattoo of Elvis" obviously has a ghost in his family who begs to break a taboo.

Horror-erotica goes one step further than gothic, because it dares the reader to be sickened and aroused simultaneously, senses betrayed. Tom Caffrey found that his story "Absolution" caused a lot of controversy for the same reason that the film, *The Night Porter,* was damned: unforgettable and yet off-limits. When a writer combines sexual release with violence, incomprehension, and inhumanity, it bursts every romantic bubble in the book. But since when did real sex get a feel-good money-back guarantee? Never in real life, only in fake virtuous literature.

One major department of erotic truth-telling that has only opened up in the past decade is the arrival of sexual speech that is not predicated on the white American experience. As much as the "dark exotic" sexual genre has been exploited for maximum titillation, it is typically told from the either earnest or transparently repressed view of the segregated white viewer.

The old-fashioned voices of black, Latin, and Asian communities tend to condemn pornography as something that only white devils and inferiors do. My favorite example was last year when the Chinese government had the first big sex fair in modern China, yet all the models in their convention literature and videos were Caucasian.

I have some black female friends who go off on seasonal girls-only retreats to read their erotic poetry and short stories, dance for each other, put together the wildest and most dedicated sexual performance. They insist that they wouldn't publish this stuff in the mainstream (read: white) world, that to go public would just reinforce every ugly stereotype about brown-sugar mamas or unbearable bulldaggers.

But I think the stereotypes stick around in their dated little rut because nobody sticks their head out and tells the truth, whatever it is. It is a matter of artistic leadership, and who's going to take the lumps for being the pioneer. Anne Wallace's "Miranda . . ." and Al Lujan's "Indio" speak out of the barrio. Trac Vu's exquisite memory is from Vietnam, and Le Shaun takes no prisoners in "wide open," which I heard her rapping before I read it.

It is relatively easy to break new ground in erotic writing, since usually only the most banal settings and situations have been recycled. The atmosphere of a photographic darkroom, a bike messenger garage, a prison tryst (from Annie Regrets, Corwin Erickson, and Susan Musgrave, respectively) were all the hooks that led me into unique intimate situations between two people. When Paul Reed tells the story of a gay man's first time with a (bisexual) woman, or Tsaurah Litzky begs for her lover to come back; when Susan St. Aubin's anti-hero can only dream of his lover's ears, and when Raye Sharp and Anna Nymus create the surprised and the surpriser—believe me, the best part is all in the details.

A couple of these stories made me cry. That's an irresistible sign. Many of them made me laugh out loud, and that's pretty much of a shoo-in, too. I've got the whole world of critics on my side when it comes to laughing, crying, or pissing in my pants. What a great story, everyone agrees.

But I have to warn you, these stories aren't content to toy with your tears or the perspiration on your brow. This is a garden that begs to be laid down in, a burning rose bush that draws you in too far to discern what's above or below the waist. Damn right it's literature—I'll leave you to reward yourself.

Susie Bright

LOW-CUT

Lisa Palac

I MET CHERYL through an ad in the newspaper. It said something like, "Very attractive blonde looking for female playmate. Boyfriend wants to watch." Yeah, my boyfriend wanted to watch, too.

The first time I tried answering a personal ad looking for a blue-moon girlfriend, I was single and I didn't have very good luck. I wrote a short letter giving my name and phone number and enclosed a picture. It was one of those black-and-white photo booth prints of me dressed in black, smiling. I hand-colored it, made it kind of arty. I never got a response. Maybe she chickened out. Maybe she thought I was a dork. I tried again with a different ad and ended up meeting this softball chick in a sports bar. I knew it would never work. I hated sports. Plus she had bad skin.

After I started seeing Greg, I decided to try it again.

(Greg was the first guy I ever watched a porn movie with, and every one we rented was a "lesbian" one. He was an all-girl action connoisseur. He never picked a tape that had any guys in it, and I can't say I minded. Women turned me on and besides, who wanted to see a bunch of ugly guys with nothing going on but big dicks?) One night, after a sweaty session in front of the VCR, he said, "I'd like to see you do it with another woman."

Now some women might interpret such a fantasy as the product of a selfish, macho mind, doped up on too much fake lesbian porno. But I thought of it more as classic, bedrock eroticism. I know that watching two women fuck each other is no doubt the number-one hetero male fantasy, but I like it, too. Until Greg's brilliant idea, I'd slept with one woman, and it was a lot less gymnastic than any porn video. I was amazed by how soft her skin was; it really was like silk. While we were doing it, I kept thinking, "Girls are so soft. Do I feel that soft to her?" I was drowning in her silky water. I liked feeling her nipples in my mouth, the way her cunt smelled. Her body was peculiar and familiar at the same time. And I liked the challenge of figuring out how to hold it in my hands and make it work, how to make her come, even though I'd spent hours toying with my own circuitry! Greg's interest was a green light for me; he encouraged my desires. So rather than accuse my boyfriend of having a sick, Bruce Seven-induced fantasy, I decided to live it out.

Finding a woman who will just go home with you and your boyfriend, who, depending on the angle looks like either Jeff Goldblum or a demented rabbit, isn't the easiest thing in the world. It's not like in the movies where everyone just wants to fuck and suck at the drop of a hat. Greg and I spent lot of time in bars saying, "She's cute," or "How about her?" but that's as far as it got. I got restless waiting for that perfect pick-up moment, where she'd start rubbing my thigh and I'd let her mess up my lipstick while Greg silently paid the tab and guided us to his apartment. Deep down, we were both nervous and neither one of us had the courage to act.

So I wrote another letter. I picked an ad where having sex was clearly the goal. I laid it on thick this time, but didn't send a photo. I hated giving away good pictures of myself that I never got back. A few days later, Cheryl called. She had this cigarette-smoking, tough-girl voice, but it was sexy, and she was very matter-of-fact. She was young, early twenties, same as me, and she gave me a detailed physical description of herself (height, weight, bra size, always emphasizing very attractive) and let me know that fucking "her old man" was out of the question and she wouldn't lay a hand on mine. We arranged to meet at my favorite snotty art bar, the New French Café. "You'll know me because I'll be wearing a black jumpsuit," she said. Jumpsuit. My heart sank a bit. The only place you could get a black jumpsuit was at the Army surplus or Frederick's of Hollywood. I imagined her to look like one of the go-go dancers on *Laugh-In*: big hairsprayed curls and mondo cleavage stuffed in a low-cut, bell-bottomed spandex capsule.

I wore black, too: leather jacket, dark sweater, jeans. And I think my hair was black then, fashionably unbrushed and matted with gobs of gel. Greg showed up in his usual plaid flannel shirt over some rock T-shirt, which may have been "The Cramps: Can Your Pussy

Do the Dog?," his long dark hair equally shocked with styling goo. He had "I can't believe you're doing this" pasted on his face. I ordered a glass of Côte du Rhône; he had scotch. It was a late afternoon in winter, still light out. I usually tried to wake up before the sun went down again.

I picked out Cheryl like a cherry when she walked in. Cleavage and everything, just like I pictured it. And she was very attractive in a working-class way. Her sexy outfit was expected but sincere. She wore dark eye shadow and bright pink lipstick. I watched heads turn, not because she was that beautiful, but because nobody would come to the New French dressed like that. When she sat down, I wanted to reach over and touch her downy, powder-puff skin. Her man, on the other hand, was a greaseball. He had a bad haircut and a big gut and a mustache. Let's call him John. I was very thankful for the anti-cock swap arrangement.

Just like on the phone, Cheryl got right down to business. She basically said that she and John, let's call him, answered a lot of ads and were always looking for new thrills. She wanted the four of us to go out to dinner one night, to "get to know each other," and then we'd go back to their house and do it. Greg suggested he bring along something from his girl/girl collection. "But he don't touch me and you don't touch him," she reiterated. Thank God.

She dictated a very particular dress code: "I want you to wear something on top that's tight and really low-cut and a miniskirt with thigh-high, spike-heeled boots. Stockings and a garter belt, of course." Uh, okay. I didn't own any of these items, except the miniskirt, but I didn't want to tell her that. While Cheryl was dressing me up like a total slut, the guys were talking and snorting, bonding in that guy way. I think they were talking about beer. We made plans for the following Sunday.

The next night, I got a call from Cheryl asking if I'd like to come over to their house and spend some time getting to know each other, as she put it. I said okay, but told her that Greg was working and so I wasn't gonna do anything, if that's what she had in mind, without him there. They picked me up and we drove to their Minneapolis suburban home. In the car I noticed that Cheryl was wearing panty hose; not cotton tights or colored stockings, but these No Nonsense suntan-colored panty hose. The dinosaur of hosiery. I felt bad for mentally picking on her panty hose, but they were so strangely out-of-date. I began to wonder if I could really get to know a person who wore beige panty hose.

Their house was tiny with paneling in the living room and a lime-green shag carpet. I sat down at the kitchen table in a chair with a wrought-iron back and puffy, flowered vinyl on the seats. John handed me a Schlitz. He asked me what I did for a living. "I'm in film school," I said. He worked in a factory, I think. Then Cheryl wanted to show me some of the other responses she'd gotten to her ad.

She and I went into the bedroom, and she plopped a big cardboard box on the bed. One by one, she showed me photos and letters from the girls who wanted to play with her. It had never even occurred to me to send a naked picture of myself, much less one with my legs spread wide and a dildo in my pussy. I was shocked, simply shocked, that people would send this hard-core, possibly incriminating stuff through the mail to some stranger at a P.O. Box. No wonder I didn't get lucky the first time around. The letters were just as explicit, out-lining how much they loved to eat pussy or how they wouldn't do anal, and of course how disease-free and very attractive they were. Well, who's going to admit their unattractive piggishness, right?

As we were looking through the stuff, Cheryl started rubbing my leg. Her skirt was hiking up her thighs and I now saw that she was not, in fact, wearing panty hose, but flesh-colored nylons and an industrial-strength garter belt. I couldn't decide if that was better or worse than the panty hose. When she saw me looking at her legs, she leaned over and kissed me. Her mouth was soft and I liked the way she kissed. Then, out of nowhere, greasy John appeared in the doorway, hand on his crotch. I gotta go, I said. She reminded me about the clothing requirements for our date. I admitted that I didn't have any thigh-high boots, so she made me try on several pairs of hers. I hoped for black, but the only ones that fit were an ugly tan with a thick broken heel. It was hard to feel sexy in tan boots, but I reminded my-self to be open to new experiences.

A few days later I got another call from Cheryl. She wanted to take me lingerie shopping. Immediately I flashed on one of those contrived Penthouse-type let-ters where two innocent girls are seduced in the dress-ing room of the bra department by some horny saleslady. But I did need that stocking and garter belt get-up, so I agreed to join her.

We ended up at a suburban mall, but neither Cheryl nor any of the salespeople seemed the least bit inter-ested in attacking me. In fact, Cheryl seemed quite non-chalant about the whole thing. She didn't even ogle as my naked breasts slipped from bra to bustier. She sat on a tiny stool outside the dressing room, dryly indicating her preferences. I picked out a white, lacy set. "Now remember," she said, "always put the stockings and garter on first, then the panties. That way you can take the panties off without having to undo everything." On the way home she told me how she occasionally worked as a stripper, both in clubs and at bachelor parties, and about some of the other personal ad experiences she'd had. "But you know, I'm really just looking for a friend," she said. "Someone I can hang out and do stuff with, like go bowling."

The Sunday of our sordid affair finally arrived. I spent the afternoon getting dolled up in my new clothes. I piled on the eyeliner and made my hair really big with lots of spray. I remembered to put the panties on over the garter belt and tried to get as much cleavage going as possible. Ah, the boots. Now I was painted. I felt like an actor in an absurd and darkly erotic theatrical performance. My prior meetings with Cheryl had been the rehearsals for opening night. And while the meticulously premeditated sex scene gave me a sense of what to expect, it also sliced off bits of spontaneity. I wondered if I might feel the same calculated degree of excitement if we'd picked up a woman in a bar.

Cheryl and John picked us up at my place in the early evening. The deal was that Cheyl would pick a place to have dinner. I assumed it would be someplace nice, and most importantly, dark and mood-setting. Instead we ended up at a family restaurant, a Denny's knockoff, right at the highway exit. It was blindingly bright, with glowing orange booths and plenty of screaming children. The place didn't even have a liquor license. I teetered through the door in my high-heeled boots, looking like a Hollywood whore, and feeling the burn of a thousand eyeballs. I wanted to explain to every single patron that, hey, I don't usually look like this, but that would have been impractical. The waitress sneered at us and I knew she was thinking, Hookers. Dinner couldn't have been over fast enough.

Back at their house, I finally started to unwind with a few slugs off of a Schlitz. John rolled a joint while Greg fiddled with the VCR, cueing up his favorite vibrator scene. Then the doorbell rang. Cheryl put her eye to the peephole and screamed, "Oh shit, it's my dad!" She waved her arms insanely at John, indicating he should hide the pot and mouthed, "Turn that fucking thing off!" to Greg. "Hi, Daddy," I heard her say, sweet as pie, when she opened the door. Daddy had come, tool set in hand, to fix something. Cheryl gave him a quick kiss on the cheek, then made a few frantic introductions.

"So how do you know Cheryl?" he asked me. My mouth hung open for about ten years, until Cheryl made up some lie. Bowling. Or maybe it was a party. "Well, seeing as you have company, I guess I'll come back tomorrow to fix that thing," he said. Oh no, stay, I thought. Stay for a porno movie and watch your little girl get banged! I held my breath until he left.

I don't remember how long it took for everyone's edginess to dissolve but eventually Cheryl and I ended up in the middle of the living room floor on a blanket in our underwear. Greg and John sat quietly on opposite ends of the sofa, watching. We made out for a while, slowly peeling off each other's bras. With the new panty trick I'd learned, the stockings and garter stayed in place, although I actually tried to take my stockings off at one point because they started bagging at the knee and I thought it looked rather unappealing. "Keep them on," Cheryl whispered in my ear.

Exactly how I licked and sucked her or what she did to me is a melted-down dream, except for this: She brought out a strap-on dildo and told me to use it on her. It was a slender, pink rubber cock, attached to two white elastic straps. The dildo itself was hollow and looked oddly clinical. (It wasn't until much later that I learned it was really a penis-extender, designed so a man could slip his cock inside of it and make himself "bigger." Makes me kinda wonder about John.) I didn't want my naïveté to show, so I stuck my legs through the straps and Cheryl got on all fours. Just as I was getting the hang of it—I mean it's not very easy trying to maneuver a piece of plastic that's belted to your crotch with a couple of rubber bands—one of the strands snapped.

"Oh, that happens all the time," John said and held out his hand in an offer to fix it.

I didn't have a mind-blowing orgasm. I don't think Cheryl did either. We just stopped, I think, when Cheryl detected a feeble moan from John. Strangely enough, neither one of the guys took out their cocks and beat off during the show. Etiquette, perhaps. John didn't whip it out, so Greg decided he wouldn't either. But in the end, John did have a large wet spot on the front of his jeans and had obviously been doing some discreet grinding.

Our good-byes were polite. I expected to have trouble tearing myself away from such a landmark moment, but what I really wanted was to be alone with Greg. We called a cab and went home.

I didn't hear from Cheryl the next day or the next week or in the following months. After all that, the pornographic reality just folded up into an odd and not particularly sexy memory. Occasionally I'd find a snapshot from the event floating in the front of my brain and I'd say to Greg, "Remember when her dad came over?" or "I can't believe that dildo broke."

Nine months later, I went to interview my first porn star, Bunny Bleu, for my cut-and-paste xerox sex 'zine, "Magnet School." I walked into the adult bookstore on Hennepin Avenue and through the crowd saw Bunny having her picture taken with a fan. She and another woman were standing with their backs to the camera, arms around each other's shoulders. "Okay, on the count of three turn your heads around and smile," said the Polaroid photographer. When the flash went off, Bunny turned and smiled and so did Cheryl. Then Cheryl turned completely around and she was very pregnant.

She waddled over to me and gave me a hug. "I'm just here havin' a picture for John because he's in jail," she said. "DUI. He cracked up the car really bad, but he's okay. Baby's due in a few weeks. You're doing a sex magazine, huh? Send me a copy when it's finished."

Her world was so unlike mine. The panty hose we wore, the kitchen chairs we sat on, the liquor we drank, the way she said old man and I said boyfriend, the places we hung out, all screamed class difference. We had nothing in common except one thing: the desire for sexual adventure. But sometimes, that's enough.

DADDY

James Williams

WHEN I WAS a callow young man I was sure I'd make a good father because I was soo-o-o fond of little kids. They were inherently sweet, I often said, full of possibilities, and innocent as clouds. Some of my friends who were parents regarded me as a unique sort of loony, as if I'd just announced for the presidency; others believed I was merely infantile or uninformed. A few ignored my romantic effusions altogether. Eventually someone would remark on the economy, foreign hostilities, or reincarnation, and conversation would resume.

When one spring I finally did get married—the last of my crowd to do so by a half dozen years—the love of my life and apple of my eye presented me with a bouncing pair of ready-made two-year-olds, one pink and one blue. This, I asserted with my cheeks flushed and my eyes aglow, was what I had been born for: *Daddy.* Somehow the word just seemed right.

Throughout the summer I rushed home from my job to be the first adult male at the local park, pushing my double stroller with my darlings freshly turned out in brand-new shirts and shorts (or coats and hats depending on the weather), bright balloons and Mylar trailers streaming from their chariot's plastic fretwork, a waterproof sack of diapers, powders, unguents, and balms, and bottles full of apple juice slung across its handlebars. Women whose children *were* their work took note, and men who hated Sundays thought I was a traitor: *Chill out,* a younger one confided to me at the swings, *you're gonna get a reputation.* One day I found another man trying to let the air out of my stroller's solid rubber tires.

At home, I fed the kids, gave them their baths, wrapped them in huge terry-cloth sheets with their names embroidered in contrasting colors, read them bedtime stories in the fading light, then tucked them in, whispering sweet nothings in the holy whorls of their baby ears. Finally I returned to the woman whose labors had given me so much happiness.

Carin was no stranger to the simple joys of motherhood. She'd dropped an older couple of whelps in the years before we'd met, and had sent them off to be raised by their fathers in a pair of far-off lands. She loved birthing babies so much I never knew when she'd do it again.

One evening after the kids had gone to sleep, my honey-lamb and I sat alone on the porch of our modest suburban home beneath a sky full of nighthawks.

"What is it about babies," she asked, "that makes you go gaga?"

I sighed a deep, contented sigh. I could feel that my lips made a moue of a smile, and the skin of my nipples tingled.

"Is it their tenderness? Their helplessness? Their warm and hopeful natures? Or is it their soft skin? The possibilities residing in their futures? The tabulae rasae that they seem to be?"

I had never had children of my own, and had always wanted to. My smile grew slightly melancholic and my lips began to fall. "It's all of that, Carin. It especially has to do with their innocence, and the trust they place in me. I love to be trusted as deeply as that, and the best way I know to receive that trust is to be a Daddy. And what is required to be a Daddy is kids."

Carin buffed one fingernail with a thumb. "*Any* kids?"

A few days later when I rushed home from work the kids were not at home—but Carin was, sitting in a largish playpen full of dolls and bright soft plastic things. She was wearing rubber pants stuffed with diapers and a soft white cotton smock with little yellow ducklings waddling around its borders. The matching bib had yellow letters spelling out her name.

"Carin?" I asked, startled enough to leave the door ajar.

"Gaa," she answered, "goo. Daddy." And she held her arms up for me, elbows akimbo, one pudgy hand clutching the ruptured neck of an ancient Cabbage Patch doll.

Slowly I approached the playpen, bent down, and

lifted her out. "Darling," I said as the doll fell away, "you're wet."

Carin cooed and burbled in my ear as I carried her to the dining table and laid her down upon its cotton cloth. She seemed entranced by the glass crystal teardrops in the chandelier above her, tinkling in the breeze from the open door. I lifted her bottom with one hand and pulled the rubber pants down with the other. The sweet pungent odor of milk-and-apple-juice urine pricked my nostrils. I unpinned the diapers and dropped them, along with the rubber pants, into a bucket someone had thoughtfully left beneath the sideboard.

Above it, on a shelf, I found a bowl of warm water; a soft, clean towel; and a pile of fresh, large diapers. I soaked the towel and wrung it out, then gently bathed Carin's closely shaved pink pudendum. She giggled with unashamed delight, although her eyes stayed fixed on the chandelier where sunlight shattered into all its hues.

After I dried her, and powdered her, and diapered her back up, I lifted Carin in my arms. Face-to-face with me she laughed and pinched my nose. I was at a loss, though. Could I take my grown-up wife to the park spilling out of a double-sized baby stroller, dressed in diapers as if she'd lost her mind?

I shrugged. War, disease, and famine were decimating the world's overblown population, but I was still a Daddy.

People gave us lots of room as I wheeled my little girl past the duck pond. She shrieked and pointed her hand excitedly at the fat birds that scurried clumsily from our path, and bounced in her seat when she heard the bells from the ice cream cart. I bought her a little cone and watched with glee as she relished the cold concoction, smearing it on her face and hands and bib. When she finally threw the cone down I took it and tossed it in the trash, then spit on a napkin and tried to rub the worst of the stickiness from her hands and face. But Carin wrinkled her nose and scrunched up her eyes and pulled away from me. And when I forced the issue, as any parent should, she began to cry. So I made a quickie job of it and said, "See? All done. Okay?" For a minute or so she looked at me suspiciously, as if unsure I could be trusted. But then she seemed to forget all about the incident.

The sun had started to set and the first nip of fall was in the air, so I turned our stroller around and made for home. There I fed her, and while I drew her bath I took off Carin's stained smock, soiled diapers, and disheveled socks, and tickled her where she lay on the dining table. Carin kicked and laughed and tried to push my hand away as it found the special places in her belly that made her jump and leap like a summer trout. But I could see that she was growing tired. I didn't want this special day to be marred by any crankiness, so I playfully lifted her up toward my shoulder and swung her back and forth as I carried her to the bath. I tested the water with my elbow and very gently set her down, splashing her limbs and stomach before settling her in the tub. After her bath I dried her with two towels, then powdered and diapered and rubber-pantsed her for the night, and carried her to the children's bed.

It was the middle of the night when I heard my darling cry. I leapt from between my lonely matrimonial sheets and into my slippers, and pulled on my robe as I ran across the hall.

Carin coughed as if just a little colicky, so I understood there was no need for me to be distressed. Nonetheless, I held her in my arms and rocked her for a while, singing gentle songs about soft winds and friendly, furry animals until her little snores told me she'd fallen back asleep.

As I laid Carin back in bed, her nightshirt bunched up and bared the bottoms of her milk-and-honeyed breasts to my kindly, fatherly gaze. Lest she catch a chill from uneven temperatures, I pushed the shirt up so it formed a bowl beneath the tender hollow at her throat. I seemed to sense her lifeblood quicken there, and her breath almost came faster: still she slept. I let my eyes caress and linger on the pale disks of her nipples, which perked up and hardened as if my fingers had touched them. She moaned in her sleep and stretched her arms above her head.

Pale and soft in the Mickey Mouse nightlight's glow, her breasts jiggled. Mounds of cream, I thought. Thick, warm gelatin frappe. Meringue. For just a moment I wondered what the babies had tasted when they nursed. Then I bent my head to suckle, and she rolled back and forth and the little bed shook violently.

A wedge of moon had risen and its light lay like a finger on the windowpane, along the futuristic planes and classic dolls and Legos scattered on the floor, up the footboard of the bed beside me, up her thigh that the soft peach cotton blanket had uncovered as it fell. More curious than prurient, as if I had all the time in the world, I took off Carin's rubber pants and diapers, and I marveled. Her hairless pudendum did not look shaved at all: it looked innocently prepubescent, virginal, and calm.

Then the moonlight pointed out the way, reddening and widening as it occupied the window altogether, spilled bright light across the floor, and slid between her legs. Her thighs parted as if on cue. She sucked and bit and nibbled on her thumb; her little lips were glistening with dew.

I traced the moonlight with my breath, in and out and up and down, imagining my wife's body was a child's. My head felt airy, as if I'd fallen asleep. I seemed to look down upon myself and her from the corner of the room where the ceiling met the distant wall. The way I saw her she was very small; her lips were parted like her thighs. When I thought of her as babylike she pushed her hips to meet me. First a finger; two; then three. I woke with my fist at the door of her womb.

The next morning, as I was trying to feed Carin breakfast, tradespeople started ringing the bell. It never occurred to me not to answer: the newsboy came to collect his change, the gas man wanted to read the meter, Jehovah's Witnesses sought to save my soul, the mailman left a postcard from the twins' grandfather saying they were having a glorious time together. Though Carin kept behaving like a baby in most respects, and none of my visitors seemed nonplussed, the presence of strangers also provoked in her a quite ungirlish, quite unsubtle display of sultry and seductive gurgling and mewing and tugging on the fibers of her clothes.

When momentarily we had peace again, between the missionaries and whatever plague the Lord next planned to send, she held out her arms all speckled with milk-besotted cornflakes to signal she was ready to be lifted from her chair. As I settled her against my hip, she started grinding hers, and making guttural sounds low down in her throat. She pressed her baby face up to my neck and sucked on the soft hollow beside my carotid artery. I grew instantly erect, and my bathrobe sash fell open.

Carin had always been profoundly erotic. Not only did she achieve each of her three pregnancies with a separate man, she also had a lengthy history of affairs and sexual friendships with both men and women. For example, she had taken up with me while married to a different man and living in a one-bedroom home with his mistress. During our prenuptial fling she more than once arrived at my door with any of several sexual companions in tow, and she was quite frank about the guests she occasionally entertained while I perambulated the twins about the park. Anything that shook— cars, trains, planes, motorcycles, horses, vibrators, hotel beds with magic fingers, food processors, joy buzzers, ancient elevators, earthquakes—anything might set her off on an orgasmic escapade. I more than once watched her shudder to a halt in broad daylight on a city street while walking past a road crew's jackhammer.

I knew my wife was a woman of vast sexual experience who had as well a vast sexual hunger. I also knew that if I did not allay her appetite, she would make certain one or another of our next visitors did. I harbored no illusions about being able to contain or limit her erotic life, but I did not want rumors about this particular baby set loose in the streets of our little town, pulling on the grown men's pants.

I did not stop to wipe the cornflakes off her arm,

therefore, or change the reality our life together had recently become. I simply carried Carin to our marriage bed and lay us down together there, and held her in the crook of my arm. As if she had cats' claws, she kneaded the skin on my belly and chest. Her hips pushed up and down on me. With an instinct that would have seemed preternatural in another child, she scuttled down my body to find the nipple of my one hard teat and started to nurse in earnest. When I could tolerate this milking no longer I slid from her mouth, knelt above her, and placed myself in her hands instead. Immediately she inserted me into herself and rocked and shook and rubbed and jumped and howled and laughed and cried at once, and her body convulsed repeatedly for several long minutes. Just before she relaxed again and settled down, for one brief shining moment my grown-up wife looked up at me. She licked her lips lasciviously and winked, and as her eyes began to flutter shut she smiled at me and whispered, "Daddy."

INDIO

Al Lujan

Don't roll your eyes at me
I was just trying to tell you that I thought perhaps,
Maybe, I was possibly starting to fall in love with you
Pinche coward
You don't know me or my people

I WAS TEN the first time I told a man that I thought, perhaps, maybe, I was possibly starting to fall in love with him. Indio was his name. He was in Big Hazard, a gang in my barrio in East Los Angeles. He was my sister's old man, she stole him from a chola named La Payasa. He was a fine white cholo. He had the first blue eyes I'd ever looked into that weren't on television. The only blue eyes in my barrio. Hair like dawn's golden blaze. Slicked back, Tres Flores pomade. Crude tattoos down his veiny forearms. Big Hazard. Done in Juvenile

Hall. All those fine cholos did Juvi. His teeth looked like those bright white Chiclets they sell at the border. They sparkled when he smiled, which was hardly ever. They crowned his fuzzy goatee. Red bandanna, white tee, khakis, Converse, always. Muthafuckin' fine white cholo.

My sister and I would stay up late talking, listening to 45s and making up dances. I remember I made up this dance to *I'm Your Puppet*. It was a cross between these Balinese dancers I'd seen on a film at school and that cholo posturing that still turns me on. It never really caught cn, not with the cholos, not with the Balinese. Not even with those fucking dorks on *American Bandstand.*

My sister practiced on me what she would say to Indio later. And showed me how they'd kissed tongue and all on her life-sized Pink Panther stuffed toy. Bumping and rolling, all motion. I took notes. And like that song said, I beat her to the punch.

He was waiting for her after school by the flood control building off Soto Street by my house. My sister, that skag, she was always in detention at Santa Teresita Catholic school for girls. Girls tripping down that road to cholahood. Hell by tenth grade, she was already teasing her hair, reeking of Aqua Net. She plucked out all her eyebrows and drew them back even higher than La Payasa. And La Payasa was chola-controlla.

So I hung out with him between buildings, listening to oldies on his portable 8-track. He pulls out this wrinkled pinner, lights it.

"*Quieres? Compra,* just kidding, holmes. *Toma.*"

I took the joint, put it to my mouth and took a puff. I really didn't inhale, I mean I was only ten, I just held it in my mouth. Then it all spilled out. I told him that I thought perhaps, maybe I was possibly starting to fall in love with him, and threw in that I thought he was the toughest and cutest cholo in Big Hazard, even if he was a white boy. Those were my sister's words really. I told you I took notes.

He started laughing. Heh Heh Heh . . . Heh Heh Heh.

And that hurt. It hurt worse than, woooosh, El Chicote, the electrical cord used to discipline my brother and I when we were acting like *maníacos*.

So he laughed, for a while, and stopped and asked, "You really think so, holmes?"

"*Claro que sí*," I squeaked back.

He leaned over and put his mouth on mine. I reached up, put my hands on his face and pulled him into me. Like I'd seen my sister and the Pink Panther do. He put his tongue in my mouth, filled it. I had to put my hands on his waist because I felt drunk, drunk. He pulled open his Pendleton, folded it, placed it down. He took my hand and guided it around his torso. I felt his hard stomach, his hard chest. I even felt the hair under his arms, of which I had none. He led my hand down to the front of his khakis. And there with my trembling hand, I felt my first hard dick. Also, which I had none of . . . yet. With his free hand he pulled my head down.

A sudden yank at my hair and I was floored. My sister was over me, scratching my face with her knee in my gut. Nearby, my mother, crying, looking skyward, "*Por qué, Jesús, por qué?*"

Blood ran down my face and spotted the sidewalk like black cherry stars. Blood, the color of my birthstone. Through my tears I could see my brother running toward Indio with a switchblade in his hand.

This was, of course, before the pop of a pistol was such a familiar sound in the barrio. Shit, I would have been the first widowed, pre-teen, gringo-boyfriend-stealing, queer bastard in East Los Angeles. Maybe not.

Indio took off up Soto Street, my brother right behind him, dodging fat women with fat children. And just vanished.

MY FAMILY moved to South Gate. My sister ran away from home. My brother kicked my ass just about every day. *Puto, pinche maricón,* fucking sissy, became my new nicknames. My abuelita, who used to call me *mijo,* "my son," now referred to me as *jotito,* "little fag." This was my grandmother. But worse than all of that shit, much worse, I never got to see Indio, that fine white cholo, again.

> So the next time I try to tell you that I thought, perhaps,
> maybe I was possibly starting to fall in love with you,
> don't roll your eyes at me, man!
> Just look deep into mine.
> Then look over your shoulder.

DATING FOR DOLLARS

Scarlett Fever

I PAUSE AT the doorway to the dining room of Lutèce, allowing the room a good viewing. My deep purple spandex dress fits like a wet suit in the few places it covers. One arm bare and supple, the back cut low and the sides cut high. My nipples straining against the material manage to rise to the occasion of all the attention. The maître d' smiles and motions, across a sea of perfectly coiffed silver heads, for us to follow. The gentle murmur of polite conversation slows as all heads turn in concert. I hear the whisper of pearls across black velvet, the subtle intake of breath and the click of my own three-inch heels as they watch me stroll across the room. The maître d', delighted by the reaction I provoke, takes his time as he walks me to the center before turning to direct us to a semi-private corner banquet. I feel the watery eyes of flaccid, ruddy-cheeked men gaze

surreptitiously while the eyes of the wives shoot conde-
scending arrows of disgust. I enjoy these reactions im-
mensely. I don't belong here. My dress is too tight, my
hair too short and too red, and my class too low. So I
take pleasure in the fact that I am here. My date for the
evening seems to feel only slightly uncomfortable in his
conservative suit and foolish grin. Perhaps it's the simple gold wedding band he wears that causes him discomfort. Or maybe he wasn't prepared for the reaction
my appearance here would create. Whatever it is, it's
his problem now. He has already given me my fee for
the evening, the two hundred dollars I would have
made had I worked tonight in the topless club where
we met.

I slip next to him on the brocade cushions of the ban-
quette, our thighs touch, and I can feel the heat rise as
his face colors slightly. His uneasiness excites me. We
share several martinis before dinner and he begins to
relax, asking the same questions they all do.

"Do you like your work?" *Oh sure. When I was little I
always wanted to grow up, be naked, and spend my time
drinking cheap champagne in dives with assholes like you.*

"Do you like being naked in front of strangers?" *See
question number one.*

"Do you get turned on with everyone watching?" *If I
was turned on do you think I would be charging you for my
time, jerk?*

"Does your family know?" *Yeah, they brag over holiday
dinners to my cousin the judge and my uncle the dentist.
They're thinking of including photos in the next family
newsletter.*

"Have you ever done it with a woman?" *Have you?*

I tell him what he wants to hear and I watch as tiny

BEST AMERICAN EROTICA 1995

beads of sweat begin to appear around his hairline. There is a moment of relief for him as the waiter comes for our order. I lean over to whisper in his ear, one hand resting between his legs; my breast rubs against his arm.

"I don't know what I want. I'd like you to make all my decisions tonight." I leave my arm, hand, breast on him while he orders, feeling his erection growing.

"Thank you," I whisper as the waiter retreats, "I knew you could take care of me." I let my hand brush across his cock as I sit up and fish the olive out of my martini. He smiles and slips his hand between my legs as I suck the vodka off the olive. I cross my legs, trapping his hand, "Not here . . . after dinner."

We have a sumptuous dinner, all the time being watched by the proper ladies whose glares he tries to avoid and the jealous men whose eyes I catch and smile directly at, while my hand tortures his erection beneath the linen tablecloth. The women are feeling self-right-eous and upset, their balding overstuffed husbands think of the deflated breasts and dry pussies across the table from them and groan in desperation. My date is straining for the release of orgasm. Everyone is right where I want them to be and I am in my glory.

"Check," he calls, unable to stand the teasing another minute.

"And coffee, please," I add.

He pulls out his gold American Express card. This is what I have been waiting for all night, the pièce de résis-tance. He prepares to sign, but I haven't gotten a good enough look at the card.

"Would you pour me the last of the Cristal please, it seems a shame to let it go to waste." He reaches over for the bottle leaving me a clear view of the card. I already

40

know his name so it's merely a matter of memorizing a short series of numbers and the "member since" date. I take one sip of the champagne and excuse myself to the ladies' room before the coffee arrives.

I slip into a phone booth instead and drop in a dime. Eddie answers on the first ring; he's been waiting for my call.

"OK. Gold. Am Ex. Member since 1981." I reel off his name and the number series off the card.

"Gotta go, don't want to lose my momentum here."

"You comin' home?"

"Nah, he's still got a coupla bills pocket change I want."

"Tomorrow, then?"

"Tomorrow." Click.

They watch me again as I stride across the floor back to the secluded corner where my romeo of the moment waits. He wants to hit a hotel. He obviously can't take me home with him and doesn't even suggest my place. Saves me the trouble of coming up with a reason why we can't go there.

"I know where we can get a little blow before we settle in for the night. What d'ya think? It really makes me crazy . . ." I let my body brush full against his. He's lost, he's helpless, he's mine. I hustle him into a cab and head thirty blocks downtown and two flights up to a dark, dirty, cavernous space where I know everybody. Through a dark room with an old pool table and a couple of warped sticks into a darker room where the bar is. The liquor's cut-rate, the glasses are plastic, and the music is blaring. I belong here, he doesn't, and everyone here wants his money as badly as I do. But I have a leg up. Literally. I'm next to him on a threadbare corner couch, one leg sprawled across his lap, snaking down between his legs, pressing against the ever-present erection. My hand inside his jacket playing with his nipple as Max the Mumbler wanders over with pockets full of cocaine. My romeo pays for an eight ball, and the vampires and coke whores can smell it in the air. They slowly surround us. We are the center of this universe as long as we have the cocaine and the money. He is loving it. He's never known people like this. The red light of the club gives it all a surreal, dangerous quality, but he feels safe with me. We share our coke with his new friends: Bobby Blue Eyes, a jewel thief wanted in five states; Marco, a hundred-dollar hustler who looks like Richard Gere; Blackie, recently released from an eight-year bid she did for dismembering an Oriental gentleman friend of hers; Smilin' Dennis, Jack the Jew, Jimmy Bug Eyes. . . . The more coke we had, the more friends we had. Romeo loves it. They talk to him as if he is one of them, a nightcrawler, not just a daytime citizen anymore. I sense I'm beginning to lose control of the situation. I aim him over to one of the blackjack tables in the corner.

"I wanna play, too," I whine. He peels off a hundred dollars and settles in to play cards.

"Oh, Vincent's here," whispering in his ear, "His coke is so much better than Max's . . . please, can I? You'll see how good it is." I get an eight ball from Vincent, give romeo half a gram, and sit in for two hands of twenty-one, both of which I promptly lose.

"Too rich for my blood," as I push away from the table stretching my body out against the thin purple of my dress. I let my hand drop into his lap and caress his thigh and cock, which has now shriveled down to its original birth weight. I spend another twenty minutes or so feeding him coke and cocktails while rubbing his shoulders from behind. Letting my breast rub across the back of his head. He's losing like crazy. Everyone is happy. The house has his money, I have his money and his coke, and he has me.

"I'm gonna shoot some pool with the Mouse out front. Come get me as soon as you're ready. OK, babe?" He takes one look at the Mouse, her huge tits barely covered by the black strapless number she's got on. They seem to have a life all their own. Her hair and eyes so dark you only see her smile in this light. She slips her arm around me and I think he's going to pass out. We always get this reaction; if I can't hurt them, she can. If she can't hurt them, I can, and there's damn few citizens that can resist the combination. Her dark voluptuousness and my pale outrageousness.

"Yeah, here, take some of this," he hands me his vial of coke. "I just want to get a little even here. Turn your friend on, too."

"I plan to, baby. You ready, Mouse?"

"I'm ready," she purrs. We turn and kiss.

"Don't keep us waiting too long." We walk away, my arm around her waist, her hand on my ass.

Mouse and I enter the barely lit entranceway where the pool table is being occupied by a couple of baby pimps. We couldn't play in these dresses if the table was empty. The minute we leaned over to shoot, our respective breasts would come rolling out of our respective dresses and display themselves on the torn green felt. We keep on strolling right on out the door, down two flights, and into a cab heading toward the morning light. We sit crosstown in another after-hours club drinking cheap vodka, sharing the coke, and laughing over romeo's probable reaction when he discovers that we as well as the coke and his money are all gone. The game was fixed. The evening was fixed. And he is still only a daytime citizen. They will not let him into the club the next night or any night unless he is with someone like me. But, he can go home and tell wonderful stories to his buddies over the backyard barbecue about his wild night out with a bad girl, leaving out the embarrassing details. And I will have a new American Express card, just like his, waiting for me when I get home sometime this afternoon.

CHEAPER BY THE PAIR

Paul Reed

THIS IS A true story. The names have been changed to protect the guilty.

A couple of years ago I was perusing the "model & escort" classifieds in the back of a San Francisco gay newspaper. There amongst the scores of ads from Well-Hung Studs and Dominant Daddy-Masters, I found an ad from Bisexual Guy and His Girlfriend.

This rang a chime for me, although I'm not sure why. Up until then, I had always considered myself to be a run-of-the-mill gay boy, not interested in females, just chasing dick and butt all over town. But I had always wondered just what it would be like to toss it off with a girl. And I believed that surely, in a man's lifetime, he should have sex with a woman at least once—not out of any prescribed sex role or dictate of society, just out of curiosity.

But being a dyed-in-the-wool faggot, I really had no interest in sex with a woman. I had no idea what I would do with one, or if I could perform, or if I could even stand it.

And that's where the guy comes in, because, I figured, if there was a hot guy there, then I'd be sure to be turned on, and then we could just take it from there. If I was "faltering" a bit, then the guy could step in and take over for me, or re-arouse me, or whatever. I wouldn't be left with sole responsibility for the woman's pleasure.

So I phoned. The guy sounded really hot—a cool, rocker-dude kind of voice, very sexy. He said he was five-foot eight, 150 pounds, muscular, with a firm round butt, smooth skin, clean-shaven, and an eight-inch, very thick cock. Yum, I thought. He said his girlfriend really enjoyed having two guys to play with (I could understand that), and that she loved watching boys suck each others' dicks (I could get into that).

He said she was a dancer, five-foot four, 110 pounds, slim, with nice breasts and a firm, almost boyish bottom.

That sounded okay to me, though something about discussing a woman in objective terms made me bristle—as though it were politically incorrect, even sexist somehow—even though it's done about men all the time.

The big question for me, however, was whether or not there would be access to "the heart of the matter," her pussy. I had some idea that girls don't like to get fucked, that they only do it to accommodate men. I wondered if she'd let me fiddle around, but not actually fuck her. If that were the case, then I didn't really want to bother.

He assured me that of course each situation was different, and both he and she responded differently to different clients, but that really, nothing was out of the question.

Hot damn. So, having satisfied my questions about the dynamics of looks and circumstances, I made an appointment with them for the following Friday evening. It was going to be expensive—$250—but I had expected a high price. Everyone knows pussy costs more than cock, which is, I'm sure, because men are so willing to give it away at all times that the only reason to pay for a guy is because of convenience, urgency, or something exceptional like a fetish look, or a huge cock, or a perfect physique. But pussy has always been harder to get, I guess because women aren't supposed to use it as much, or they're supposed to protect their virtue, or because they don't like sex as much (yeah, right).

When Friday rolled around, I was a jumble of nerves, a combination of excitement, curiosity, performance anxiety, and the sheer thrill of the adventure. Trying to get any work done was hopeless, and trying to eat dinner even more so.

Their place was out in the avenues by Golden Gate Park, and it was a foggy, cool evening. "Tom" answered the door, and I was immediately put at ease because he was such a regular kind of guy—truly, he looked like your average handsome straight man, youngish, fairhaired, with that strong aquiline nose that straight boys have. The idea of messing around with him made me powerfully horny.

He invited me in to meet Claire, and that's when I got really nervous, because she was incredibly beautiful, with long brown hair, flashing eyes, and skin that looked like whipped cream. I was intimidated by her beauty.

But she was sweet enough, as was he. There was a kind of tension in the room, which Tom tried to relieve by getting me a soda, and then Claire suggested I "get comfortable," so we all began to strip. Claire was the first to get naked, and her body was really beautiful— firm, smooth, flawless skin. And, interestingly, I noticed that her pussy was shaved.

She jumped into bed and under the covers, as did Tom. Something about climbing under the covers with the two of them put me at ease—it made the encounter more like some kind of sexy slumber party, rather than a client being serviced by two prostitutes.

Of course, you can imagine what it was like—a man on one side and a woman on the other, all of us kissing and rubbing and tugging and stroking. I kept focusing on the man—partly out of habit, partly out of shyness, and partly because I just didn't know what to do with Claire. Finally, Tom asked me if I'd like to watch him fuck her, and of course I said yes, so they started fucking and thrusting and all of that.

I was rapt, getting down close to watch his hard cock slide in and out of her shaved cunt. This was really turning me on. She reached out and pulled my head between her breasts and said, "You can play with them, you know." So I began to squeeze and stroke her tits, licking and sucking on the nipples. It was just like playing with a guy's tits, only bigger and more ripe— swollen is the word.

When he stopped thrusting into her, I moved down between her legs and asked if I could just look. "I don't really know where anything is," I explained. She laughed and said, "Go ahead and look all you want."

I think it was the fact that she was shaved that made it so intriguing to me, for here was everything all laid out as clear as could be. "You can lick it if you want to," she said, and I did, tentatively at first, then with more enthusiasm.

I've always loved rimming boys, and always been squeamish because of the fear of parasite infections. But I discovered something that night—eating pussy was even better than eating ass. There was so much more to do, so many nooks and crannies. And so much less worry about exposing myself to something.

Eventually I found her clit. I wasn't sure at first, but the way she started moaning and groaning, I figured I was there. And I really got off on it, sucking and nibbling and licking. I put a finger inside her at the same time, and she started thrashing around, gasping and bucking her hips and clawing at the sheets.

Tom was sucking on her nipples and running his hands over her body. Eventually she pushed my head away and gasped that she needed a break.

"But don't you want to cum?" I asked her.

She looked astonished, then laughed. "That's what I've been doing," she said. "For a virgin, you sure know how to give head."

I think I turned bright crimson, I was so embarrassed that I hadn't realized she'd been having an orgasm. It's just that with men, there's a distinct high point, then a taste treat, then their dicks go soft. With Claire, I'd thought I was getting her close, but was waiting for some exclamatory act—like the way boys shoot cum— to declare her orgasm.

Having given her so much head, my jaw was pretty tired, and they suggested that I lie back and let them do me. Claire straddled my head and lowered her cunt back onto my face, and Tom knelt over my crotch. With her pussy on my face, I couldn't see which one of them was actually sucking my dick, but I could feel that the two of them were trading off sucking it.

And I could tell that one of them was doing a much better job than the other. One of them knew what to do, how to suck, and the inside of the mouth just felt different, better somehow. Eventually Claire rolled her cunt off my face, and I was able to determine which of them was giving the good suck job—it was Tom.

So I guess it is true what they say, that boys suck dick better than girls. But since eating pussy is so much better than rimming a boy's butthole, I guess it balances out somehow.

It was Tom who got me off, using his hand and his mouth, which is one of my favorite ways to cum. And then I sucked him off, which was a real thrill, because Claire was lying there watching as I sucked her boyfriend's dick till it shot a load of cream in my mouth.

Anyway, that's my story about the first time—and so far, only time—I've messed around with a girl. I hope to repeat the experience someday. Any takers?

30

Raye Sharpe

Pissed off doesn't even begin to describe how I felt. I didn't turn thirty *every* day; D. hadn't even sent me a birthday card, the scum. I padded to the kitchen and looked into the nearly empty refrigerator. The choices were warm milk (face creams and face lifts couldn't be too far behind), or the last of the Chardonnay. "If life begins at thirty," I thought, "well, then let's begin it in style." The wine was golden in the large goblet I emptied the bottle into. "Happy, happy," I said to myself as I downed the woody elixir.

I was supposed to call Karen to come pick me up in an hour, and I hadn't even dressed yet. I pulled the satin robe around my body and looked at myself in the window's reflection. I lifted my hair up with one hand and blew a sexy kiss at myself. I looked down at the pavement and watched the snow fall gracefully through the halo of the street lamp. I yanked open the robe, flashed, and thought, "Birthday depression be damned!"

I started at the sound of my own buzzer. "Who is it?" I growled into the intercom's speaker. No answer. "Friend or foe?" I yelled. The speaker crackled on the other end. I rushed into the bedroom, threw off the robe, and pulled on a T-shirt and jeans that were lying in a heap at the end of the bed.

I swore as I stomped down the hallway stairs, shoving my uncooperative hair out of my eyes as I rounded the last banister. I peeked around the corner at the figure in the doorway. I stood at the top step and glared down. D. smiled back at me through the window of the foyer door. I stood with my arms crossed and rested my weight on one leg. "Scum," I thought. "Where's my birthday card?" D. grabbed the doorknob and shook it to try and get in. I cocked my head to one side and slowly descended to the door.

D.'s leather coat was covered in snow, and his buzz-cut hair shimmered in the hallway light. "Let me in!" he laughed, as I stood and stared through the door's window at his reddened lips and cheeks. He was holding something behind his back with his left hand and banging on the glass with his right. I opened the door a crack and he pushed his body through, shoving me back in the process. "Get upstairs," he said.

"Forget it. You knew it was my birthday; you didn't even call me and now I've made other plans."

"I said, get upstairs." He forced my wrist behind me and pressed it into my ass while pushing me up the steps. I whipped around and got ready to throw him over the banister, but his smile stopped me. "Don't try it or I'll bend you right over this rail and spank you," he said, barely containing his laughter.

I made a face at him and ascended the stairs. As I opened my door I turned, and said, "You're out of here in fifteen minutes. Karen's on her way over."

"Yeah, right. Get inside and go sit on the couch," he spat back.

"Yes, master!" I mocked in my best *I Dream of Jeannie* imitation. D.'s blue eyes glowed as I said it. I sat down on the couch and crossed my arms over my chest. D. closed the door behind him and clicked the police lock into place. He set down a pink plastic bag as he took off his black coat. I watched him straighten his black shirt and black jeans. "Colorful choice of clothing," I joked.

He stared back at me and his serious expression broke into an amused one. I started to get up from the couch and he barked, "Sit back down and don't move until I tell you to!"

His voice was forceful enough to make me comply. I was getting even more mad now, no card, no flowers— not even a birthday kiss—and here he was, ordering me around. He went into my bedroom and yanked open the top drawer of my dresser. Bras, panties, and camisoles spilled out in pastels and primary colors. He inspected each piece, shook his head, and threw it down. He pulled the drawer out completely and emptied it on the floor. He picked through it all and delicately lifted out the red silk camisole and bikini underwear set he'd given me for Christmas. He walked into the living room with the items draped over his arm and brought the pink bag with him.

The bag jingled as he placed it on the floor. He grabbed a chair and turned it around backward facing me as he threw the lingerie on the couch. "Get up and put those on," he said as he pressed his crotch against the wooden spokes of the chair.

"Fun and games are over, pal. My friend is taking me out for my birthday, which, I may add, you have not even acknowledged. Put them on yourself and have fun. I'm not playing," I said, as I got up and attempted to swerve around him.

He blocked my way, leaned over, and kissed me full on the lips, as he lifted me off the floor. "If you don't put those on, I'll tie you to this chair and put them on you," he breathed into my ear.

I went slack in his arms. "All right, loverboy, I'll put the damn things on. But I'm telling you, fifteen minutes and you're out of here." I whipped off my clothing and lifted the camisole over my head. I pulled it down over my naked breasts and tried to cover up my erect nipples, which were pressing through the silk. I slipped on the bikinis and pulled them tight around my ass. "There, are you happy now?" I said as I sat back down on the couch with my arms crossed.

"Put your arms down," he said. I looked away from him, disgusted, and slammed my hands down beside me. He reached forward and gently arranged my hair over my shoulders. "I bought you this lingerie because you look so beautiful in red. It makes your hair and eyes look even darker than they are already," he murmured. "Sit back and relax, we've got things to talk about." He leaned down to pick up the pink bag. "We've been going out for a while now and we're getting to know more about each other over time." He reached into the bag. He smiled and pulled out a small box wrapped in shiny paper with a red ribbon. He placed it on the table and said, "I went to the store today, and got totally inspired to introduce you to a side of me you haven't met yet. It's a part of me that you're going to get to know real well." He shuffled around in the bag and pulled out a long silver chain with two leather cuffs dangling at the end. The cuffs had large buckles on one side and were joined together by a silver ring.

"You aren't serious," I said breathlessly.

He smiled back at me. "Hold out your hands." He climbed out of the chair and stood in front of me. He slipped the bands over my wrists and fastened each buckle tightly around. "Get up!" he yelled. His blue eyes flashed as he smiled. I struggled to get up and he pulled me down the hallway by the chain's leather handle. He threw me back on the bed, my hands clasped near my waist and my long hair splayed across the pillow. The crotch of his black jeans bulged as he stood back and stared. "You don't know how gorgeous you are in red," he sighed as he pulled his boots off and knelt beside me. He grabbed a handful of my hair and pulled my face up to his succulent lips. The force of his kiss pressed my head back as he gripped my ass to pull me closer to him. He ground his pelvis into mine as he pulled my hands from between us and positioned them above my head.

With my arms outstretched, the silky camisole rose just above the underside of my breasts. D.'s eyes fixated on my erect nipples. He straddled my head with his well-muscled thighs. With both of my hands clasped in his, he undid one of the waist straps and tightened it back around the bedpost. He pressed his bulge against my mouth and rubbed the zipper on my lips. I pulled against the cuffs, forcing the leather tighter on my shackled wrists. D. pulled his T-shirt off and I got a whiff of cologne mixed with salty skin. He reached up and tweaked his own nipples making me laugh at the look on his face.

"Cut it out!" he yelled. "I don't want to hear a thing from you unless you ask permission. I'll bet you thought I forgot your birthday, didn't you?" I nodded yes as he unsnapped the waist of his tight black jeans. He pulled the zipper down and opened his pants to below his hips. "Recognize these?" he asked. His erect cock was barely contained in my lace G-string that I'd left on his pillow the last time I had visited. I tried not to laugh but a giggle escaped. He kneeled back down and tried to contain his own laughter. He pulled the satin-covered elastic over the thick head of his penis. "Me, forget? Not a chance. Not only did I *not* forget, but I'm going to give you something you'll beg for all night." He pulled his jeans down and thrust his lace-covered bulge inches from my mouth. "Like what you see?"

My nipples pulsated and heat grew between my legs with the mounting excitement. I nodded yes, staring as his thick member bobbed and pressed out of the black lace G-string.

"Tell me you want it inside you."

"You know I do already," I panted.

He reached down between my legs. "You want it here, don't you? Beg me for it."

"Come on, D.," I implored, wishing he would just get down to it and fuck me.

"I said, beg me. I'll make you stare at my big dick all night if you don't."

"Please, I want your big cock to plunge into my anxious, soaking-wet pussy," I cooed.

"Tell me how wet," he whispered, leaning over and kissing down my throat. He pulled the G-string further down the shaft of his cock and rested its glistening head at my lips. He kissed over and around my bound wrists and sucked on each finger as he pulled the chain tighter.

I stuck my tongue out and licked the first drops of moisture off the head of his penis. "It's dripping on the sheets, feel underneath me," I murmured, keeping my lips in contact with the turgid skin of his shaft.

He pulled away and lifted the red satin over my breasts. He teased my nipples with his fingertips and leaned over to nibble them lightly. He bit a little harder and made me cry out. "Suck on my cock," he said, as he sat back up and took his cock in his hands. He pulled the chain's leather handle between my breasts, and rested the loop at my pussy. He slid his cock deep into my throat and made me gag from the size of him. I tried to relax my throat to accommodate him and he gently pulled out. "Take every inch of this cock right now," he said, and teased my lips with the reddened tip. He lifted my head toward him and brushed the tears that rolled down my cheeks from my gag reflex. He pulled my head to him and gently probed my mouth until his cock slid easily through my whetted lips. "Shall I tie your feet down, too?" he asked, pulling his cock out and resting it on the chain between my breasts.

"You're the master, do what you want with me," I moaned.

He ran his tongue down my body. He rolled my silk

bikini underwear over my hips and off of my legs. He
planted the top of his tongue at the cleft of my vagina as
he spread my thighs with his hands. He wriggled his
tongue through the downy folds until the top pressed
on my sensitive clit. He rubbed against it, probing
deeper and harder until my flesh pearl felt like it would
burst. He pulled the leather handle down further and
rested the loop at my vaginal opening. "That's right, I'm
the master, and right now I'm going to fuck you until
you scream," he said, just as the phone on the night
table beside us rang. D. picked up the receiver and
pressed it to my ear. I shook my head no and he
stretched his muscle-bound body over mine. "Talk!" he
commanded.

"Hello? Karen! Hi, yeah, I said I'd call, I know," I said,
trying to sound nonchalant. D. slid down my body and
started sucking on my pussy again. "You're so wet!" he
whispered as he pressed his fingers inside me.

I tried not to groan with pleasure as he continued to
thrust his thumb into me and suck on my pulsating clit.
"No, I don't think I'll be able to come out with you
tonight after all," I said.

"Tell her you're tied up," he said, coming up on his
knees and opening a condom package from the box beside the bed. He rolled it on and pressed the thick, la-
texed head of his penis through the loop of the chain's
strap handle. D. pushed the softened leather down past
the rim of the condom and pressed into my pussy so
that the attached chain was taut against my body.

I let out a loud groan as the leather strap pressed
against my clit. "No, really, Karen, that's so nice of you
to offer to come over, but I'm . . ." I tried to finish the
sentence as D.'s groin met mine with a complete thrust.

He pulled out and caused the chain to slacken and jingle. "I said, tell her you're tied up," he urged as he held himself just outside my writhing pussy.

"No, really, Karen, I just got . . . um . . . tied up here," I gasped as D. plunged all the way into me.

"That's what I wanted to hear. Now get off the phone because I'm going to fuck you so hard you're going to come all over me," he whispered, as he increased the pressure and pace of his thrusts.

"I'll call tomorrow, OK?" I said into the phone. "Maybe we can go out to lunch or something." I tried to sound convincing. D. grabbed one of the pillows beside me and shoved it under my butt. "Thanks, Karen, I will. Bye," I barely squeaked out as D. pulled the leather strap off his cock and moved the chain aside.

"Why didn't you tell her how much you love being tied up?" he asked as he held his hand over my mouth. I shifted on the bed and pulled at the restraints attached to the bedpost. He thrust in as far as he could go and forced my legs wider to fit all of him in. "I really liked the noise you made when I did *this* to you," he said louder as he pumped even faster. "Didn't you want your friend to know how hard you were being fucked?" The bed shook with every forward push. "Nod your head yes or I'll stop right now," he mocked.

I nodded as fast as I could. I was on the brink and he knew it. He positioned my hips so that the rolled edge of the condom grazed over my clit. I started making a lot of noise now, and cried out into the palm of his hand planted over my mouth.

"Tell me you want to come," he said, letting go.

"Right now!" I cried out as my climax peaked and gushed out. D. grabbed my breasts and held my nipples between his fingers as I rocked my orgasmic pussy against him.

"I'm going to come right now," he breathed into my ear. "Get ready, here it comes!" he yelled out as he gave one last thrust and threw his head back. I pulled hard on the wrist straps as he jerked his hips into me. He pumped slower and slower until the last throes wore him out. He pulled his cock out of me and rested the slick, rubberized thickness against my thigh. He lay on top of me until his breathing was back to normal. He glanced up, smiled and unbuckled the manacles. "Happy birthday," he said, pulling my hands to his lips and kissing the chafed skin. "Let's go and open your *other* present!"

BOY BORN WITH TATTOO OF ELVIS

Robert Olen Butler

I CARRY HIM on my chest and it's a real tattoo and he was there like that when I come out of Mama. That was the week after he died, Elvis, and Mama made the mistake of letting folks know about it and there was that one big newspaper story, but she regretted it right away and she was happy that the city papers didn't pick up on it. It was just as well for her that most people didn't believe. She covered me up quick.

And I stayed covered. Not even one of her boyfriends ever saw me, and there was plenty come through in these sixteen years, all the noisy men in the next room. But last week she brought this guy home from the bar where she worked and he looked like I'd imagine Colonel Parker to look. I never saw a photo of Parker, the man who took half of every dollar Elvis ever earned, but this guy with Mama had a jowly square face and hair the gray of the river on a day when a hurricane is fumbling toward us and he made no sounds in the night at all and this should have been a little better for me, really.

But Mama made sounds, and I'd gotten so used to them over the years I could always kind of ignore them and listen—if I chose to listen at all—to the men, how foolish they were, braying and wailing and whooping. At least Mama had them jumping through hoops: I could think that. At least Mama had them where she wanted them. But this new guy was silent and I hated him for that—it meant he didn't like her enough, the goddam fool—and I hated him for making me hear her again, the panting, like she was out of breath, panting that turned into a little moan and another and it was like a pulse, her moans, again and again, and finally I just went out the door and off down the street to the river.

We live in Algiers and I went and sat on a fender pile by the water and watched New Orleans across the way and I could hear music, some Bourbon Street horn lifting out of the city and coming across the river, and it's the kind of music I like to hear, at times like that. There's other music in me but his. You see, I'm not Elvis myself. I'm not him reincarnated like that one newspaper tried to make you believe. I didn't come out of my momma humming "Heartbreak Hotel," like they said.

And she almost never does this, but last night I was tired and it was my birthday and I just stuck it out and after they was finished in there, she come in to me. We have a shotgun house with shutters that close us up tight and the only place I've got is on the sofa bed in the living room, and the next room through—the path that a shotgun blast would follow from the front door to the back, which is how these houses got their name—the next room through was her bedroom and then there was the little hall with the bathroom and then the kitchen and the back door. One of her jealous boyfriends actually did fire through the house a few years ago and the doors happened to be open, but it was a blunt-nose pistol and the bullet didn't make it all the way through the house, being as there was another boyfriend standing in one of the open doors along the way. Mama come in to me after that, too, cause I'd seen it all, I carried the smell of cordite around inside me for a week after.

So she come in to me last night and maybe it was because of me turning sixteen, though she never said a word about it. Maybe it was because of this new guy staying quiet when she wasn't. But she come in and I was laying there on my back and she cooed a little and took me by the ears and fiddled with them like they was on crooked and she was straightening them and then her hands went down and smoothed flat the collar of my black T-shirt that I was sleeping in and she said to me, "How can you love a fool such as I?"

It's a good question, I think. I think Elvis sold about two million records of a song by a name like that. But she meant it. And I didn't say anything to her. She waited for me to say, Oh Mama I love you I do. But she smelled like the corner of some empty warehouse and maybe she didn't know where my daddy was or maybe even who he was but he sure wasn't the guy in there right now and he wasn't going to be the next one either or the next and the few times I said anything about it, she told me she can't help falling in love. But I didn't buy that. I couldn't. Still, I know what I'm supposed to feel for my momma: Elvis collapsed three times at the funeral for Gladys. But I'm not Elvis, and I'd stand real steady at a time like that, I think. Nothing could make me fall down. I would never fall down.

But tonight I didn't care. Tina come up to me in the hall this morning at the school and she said "I heard it was your birthday yesterday" and I said "It was" and she said "Why don't you ever talk with me, since I can't keep my eyes off you in class and you can see that very well" and I said "I don't talk real good" and she said "You don't have to" and I said "Are you lonesome tonight?" and she said "Yes" and then I told her to meet me at a certain empty warehouse on the river and we could talk and she said "I thought you weren't a good talker" and I said "I'm not" and she said "Okay." And that meant I had to figure out what to do about my chest.

Because Elvis's skin is mine. His face is in the very center of my chest and it's turned a little to the left and angled down and his mouth is open in that heavy-lipped way of his, singing some sorrowful word, but his lips are not quite open as much as you'd think they should be in order to make that thick sound of his, and his hair is all black with the heavenly ink of the tattoo and a lock of it falls on his forehead and his lips are blushed and his cheeks are blushed and the twists of his ear are there and the line of his nose and chin and cheek, and his eyes are deep and dark, all these are done in the stain of a million invisible punctures, but all the rest, the broad forehead except for that lock of hair, his temples and his cheeks and chin, the flesh of him, is my flesh.

I wanted to touch Tina. She's very small and her face is as sharp and fine as the little lines in Elvis's ear and her hair is dark and thick and I wanted to lay beneath her and pull her hair around my face, and her eyes are a big surprise because they're blue, a dark, flat blue like I'd think suede would be if it was blue. I wanted to hold her and that made my skin feel very strange, touchy, like if I put my hands on my chest I could wipe my skin right off. Tattoo and all. Not that I imagined that would happen. It was just the way my skin thought about itself today, with Tina in my mind the way she was. And you'd think there would've been some big decision to make about this. But when the time come, it was real easy. I decided to show her who I was tonight. I would show her my tattoo.

Mama used to tell me a story. When nobody was in the house and I was going to sleep, she'd come and sit beside me and she'd say do I want to hear a story and I'd say yes, because this was when I was a little kid, and she'd say, "Once upon a time there was a young woman who lived in an exotic faraway place where it was so hot in the summers that the walls in the houses would sweat. She wasn't no princess, no Cinderella either, but she knew that there was something special going to happen in her life. She was sweet and pure and the only boy who ever touched her was a great prince, a boy who would one day be the King, and he touched her only with his voice. Only his words would touch her and that meant she could keep all her own secrets and know his too and nothing ever had to get messy. But then one night an evil man come in to her and made things real complicated and she knew that she was never going to be the same. Except then a miracle happened. She gave birth to a child and he come into the world bearing the face of the prince who was now the King, the prince who had loved her just with his words, and after that, no matter how bad things got, she could look at her son and see the part of her that once was."

This was the story Mama used to tell me and all I ever knew to do at the end was to say to her not to cry. But finally I stopped saying even that. I asked her once to tell me more of the story. "What happened to the boy?" I asked her and she looked at me like I was some sailor off a boat from a distant country and she didn't even know what language I was talking.

So tonight I went out of the house and around the back and in through the kitchen to get to the bathroom. She and the Colonel Parker guy were in the bedroom and I never go in there. Never. Before I stepped in to wash up I paused by her door and there was a rustling inside and some low talk and I gave the door a heavy-lipped little sneer and a tree roach was poised on the doorjamb near the knob and even he had sense enough to turn away and hustle off. So I clicked the bathroom door shut as soft as I could and I pulled the cord overhead and the bulb pissed light down on me and I didn't look at myself in the mirror but bent right to the basin and washed up for Tina and there was this fumbling around in my chest that was going on and finally I was ready. I turned off the light and opened the door and there was Mama just come out of her room and she jumped back and her sateen robe fell open and I lowered my eyes right away and she said you scared me and I didn't look at her or say nothing to her and Elvis might could sing about the shaking inside me but I for sure couldn't say anything about it and I pushed past her. "Honey?" she asked after me.

I slammed the back door and I beat it down the street toward the river and it was August so it was still light out but the sun was softer, moving into evening, and I was glad for that. I started trying to concentrate on Tina waiting for me and I wanted the light and I wanted it to be soft and I just kept thinking about the looks she'd been giving me and I could see her eyes on me from across the classroom and they were flat blue and when they fixed on me they didn't move, they always waited for me to turn away, and I always did, and now I thought maybe she'd been seeing something important about me all along, that's why she wanted me like this. I thought maybe when I showed her who I was, she would just say real low, but in wonder, "I knew it all along."

Then I was past Pelican Liquors and the boarded up Piggly Wiggly and a bottle gang was shaping up for the evening on the next corner and they lifted their paper bags to me and I just hurried on and I could see a con-tainership slipping by at the far end of the street and I had to keep myself from running. I walked. I didn't want to be sweating a lot when I got there. I just walked. But walking made my mind turn. Mama's robe fell open and I looked away as quick as I could but I saw the center of her chest like you sometimes see the light after you turn it off, she come out of her bedroom and her robe fell open and I saw the hollow of her chest, nothing more, and when I turned away I could still see her chest and it was naked white and I wondered why

Elvis didn't appear there. She could've kept her own secret then and known his too, and there wouldn't never
had to be anybody else involved in the whole thing.

I was walking real slow now, but I could see that the
light was starting to slip away and I had better get on, if
I was going to do this thing. And I turned down the
next street and I could see the river now and I followed
it and the warehouse had a chain-link fence as high as
my house but it was cut in a few places and I found
Tina on the other side already and she saw me and she
come my way. She was wearing a stretchy top with ruf-
fles around the shoulders and her stomach was bare
and she was in shorts and I hadn't seen her legs till
now, not really, and they were nice, I knew that, they
were longer than I figured, and we both had our fingers
curled through the fence links and we were nose to
nose just about and she said, "Get on in here."

I went in and she said, "I was worried you wasn't
coming," and I found out I didn't have nothing to say to
that and she smiled and said, "I don't know this place
so well. Where should we go?"

I nodded my head in the direction of the end of the
warehouse, on the river side, and I felt a lock of my hair
fall onto my forehead and we moved off and the ground
was uneven and she brushed against me again and
again, keeping close, and I thought to take her hand or
put my arm around her, but I didn't. I wanted this to go
slow. We walked and she was saying how glad she was
that I come, how she liked me and how she was really
on her own more or less in her life and she had learned
how to know who's okay and who isn't and I was okay.

And I still didn't say nothing and I couldn't even if I'd
wanted to because I was shaking inside pretty bad and

we entered the warehouse through a door that said Danger on it and inside it was real dim but you could feel the place on your face and in your lungs, how big it was and how high, and there was that wet and rotted smell but Tina said, "Oh wow" and she pressed against me and I let my arm go around her waist and her arm come around mine and I took her into the manager's office.

The light was still coming in clear in the room and there was some old mattresses and it didn't smell too good, but a couple of the windows was punched open and it was mostly the river smell and the smell of dust, which wasn't too bad, and I let go of Tina and crossed to the window and I looked at the water, just that. The river was empty at the moment and the last of the sun was scattered all over it and there was this scrabbling in me, like Elvis went way deeper there than my skin and he'd just woke up and was about to push himself out the center of my chest. I tried to slow myself down so I could do this right.

Then I turned around to look at Tina and she must have gotten herself ready for this too because as soon as I was facing her where she was standing in the slant of light, she stripped off her top and her breasts were naked and I fell back a little against the window. It was too fast. I'm not ready, I thought. But she seemed to be waiting for me to do something, and then I thought: She knows; it's time. So I dragged my hand to the top button of my shirt and I undid it and then the next button and the next and I stepped aside a little, so the light would fall on me when I was naked there and she circled so she could see me and then the last button was undone and I grasped the two sides and I couldn't hardly breathe and then I pulled open my shirt.

Tina's eyes fell on the tattoo of Elvis and she gave it one quick look and she said, "Oh cool," and then her eyes let go of me, they let go of me real fast, like this was something she'd expected all right, but it was no big thing, there was no wonder in her voice, no understanding that this was a special and naked thing, and she was looking for the zipper on her shorts, and I was sure she was wrong about me and I hoped she'd have a son someday with a face on his chest that she would know, and then I was sliding away and the shirt was back on me before I hit the warehouse door and I didn't listen to the words that followed me but I was stumbling over the uneven ground, trying to run, and I did run once I was out the cut in the fence and I heard a voice in my head as I ran and it was my voice and it surprised me but I listened and it said, "Once there was a boy who was born with the face of a great King on his chest. The boy lived in a dark cave and no one ever saw this face on him. No one. And every night from deeper in the darkness of the cave, far from the boy but clear to his ears, a woman moaned and moaned and he did not understand what he was to do about it. She touched him only with her voice. Sometimes he thought this was the natural sound of the woman, the breath of the life she wished to live. Sometimes he thought she was in great pain. And he didn't know what to do. And he didn't know that the image that was upon him, that was part of his flesh, had a special power."

Then I slowed down and everything was real calm inside me, and I went up our stoop and in the front door and I went to the door of Mama's bedroom and I threw it open hard and it banged and the jowly-faced man jumped up from where he was sitting in his underwear on Mama's bed. She straightened up sharp where she was propped against the headboard, half hid by the covers, and she had a slip on and I was grateful for that. The man was standing there with his mouth gaping open and Mama looked at me and she knew right off what'd happened and she said to the man, "You go on now." He looked at her real dumb and she said it again, firm. "Go on. It's all over." He started picking up his clothes and Mama wouldn't take her eyes off mine and I didn't turn away, I looked at her too, and I touched the top button on my shirt, just touched it and waited, because only I could have this thing upon me, Mama couldn't have it because she'd lost it long ago and it was put on me to give it back to her and I kept my hand there and I waited and then the man was gone and the house was quiet.

It was just Mama and me and I had to lean against the door to keep from falling down.

MIRANDA THINKS SHE IS STARVING FOR LOVE

Anne Wallace

—who says no to a glass of water in the dark, waiting her turn at the washbasin, spoiled milk from her
baby sister's burp soaked through her blouse, who
bends her knees and arches her back so the small ones
will fit on the mattress near the soles of her feet and in
the crook along her spine, wanting badly to quit those
high-pitched sounds of *el espanto* ringing in her ears at
night, warning of pain, as her grandmother, long ago,
had said; whose Mamá is sewing a dress from the magazine picture of dark-haired girls in white ruffled
gowns, who will be coming out, Mamá says, *la feliz de
mi vida*, our special flower, daughter of old man Luis
who slaps her for running with Antonia, her very best
friend and lover of Jorge, cousin of bad influence, who
tongued both girls in the alley, Antonia who went all
the way with him on a cold day at the riverbed, the day

she wore her hair down long like a five-foot rope, black
and straight, no kinks, confessor to Miranda, who be-
lieves anything, who likes making something out of
nothing, who sits on the low brick wall next to the park
after school, smoothing the cloth of her long skirt, who
loves Cisco's blue eyes which lately are all over her, no
good too-light Cisco, son of Lucille, blower of hot air,
fisher for Latinas, spreader of brown legs, who hums a
tune only for Miranda, he says, the one with the black
bedspring curls, who follows him into the bushes one
day when she knows she should be home preparing for
the *quinceañera,* who giggles while crouching in the un-
dergrowth below the jacaranda limbs as he gives his
word: he'd kill for her, snapping flowers he'd picked,
breaking like nut brittle in her ears, popping buttons
and squeezing rice-colored nipples through his teeth
until plum dark, lying between her legs, holding them
wide open and daring her to face his penis; who
pinches her eyes shut for it is just as Antonia said: like
lifting corn from the boiling pot, his bone taking her
skin with him, muffling her screams against the dry
hollow of his stomach; *mi amor,* she cries, *Do you love
me?* who afterward watches the shaker of flesh throw
pennies at her feet, leaving her aching in the dirt, who
begs forgiveness, rubbing the crucifix around her neck
until she arrives home, where full in spring she gives
life to baby girl Marisol, as soft as pink palms, who she
prays will say no.

DIANA THE COURIER

Corwin Ericson

DIANA LIKED TO wear shorts as early into the season as she could. I don't know why, I was always in tights the moment it dipped below sixty. In early May, the ice was still melting in Boston. The days were beginning to stretch again and I was just starting to feel a bit jaunty after a winter of huddling in front of a space heater. I was cleaning the grime and muck off my bike, trying to shake off the torpor that had settled on me sometime back in January. Diana usually rode a nice little steel road frame she'd modified to take twenty-six-inch rims and a straight bar. She was hell to keep up with.

She and I had something of a Red Baron relationship; we never really made plans to meet but we knew where to find each other and that we'd duel when we met. She would have been a perfect flying ace. She was dashing and breathless in a sweaty sort of way. She smelled like machines and there was a fierce engine inside of her that made it seem sensible to give her more than you had. Once her legs curled around your back, you did what you could to save a little for the ride home, but it was all hers.

I had my bike upside down, resting on its seat and bar ends, working out some kinks in the chain. I gave the cranks a little shove and listened to the even click of the cassette hub and the chain whirring just so. Diana was the one who had pointed out the almost cinnamon smell of the synthetic lube we used.

Like I said, she rode like a demon but you never really saw her work. Nobody needed to get out of her way, she never seemed to risk much—the opening was right there for her every time. I know, I've tried to stay on her tail. In this weather, her legs would always blush from the wind and her own effort. The sight of her reddened legs was usually enough motivation for me to try and turn a few yellows back to reds, in pursuit of her.

I wasn't working at the time, so I'd try to meet her now and then for her lunch hour. She carried a beeper on her strap and, when I had a chance, I'd key in "LUNCH" and ride down to the pizza place that she and the other couriers used as an HQ. Usually, I'd just hang around outside and hope that she'd show—sometimes she did, other times I didn't know what she was up to. I didn't like asking her what else she did with her time. I liked to think of her as an undetainable city sylph, swooping in and out of the architecture like she was born from it.

I've seen her pull stunts that no one should have been able to get away with. She'd weave through a slow clot of traffic, blowing by the cabbies as they stewed in their perpetual sulk. There's not a rider on the planet who's got a shred of sympathy for those sullen bastards. Every cab driver is a potential homicidal sociopath when you're riding. It's such a damn pleasure to listen to them lean on their horns in impotent fury, as she glides her lycra ass right by their doughnut-bloated faces. She's just what they think they want—pure unattached feral loveliness, and if they ever try to make a grab, they get their windshield Krypto'd in.

We didn't always come back to my place. Once, in the spring, we hooked up and she never even set a foot on the pavement, just yelled, "Come on," and set off. When she'd finally slowed enough for me to catch up, we were in the Back Bay, riding down the genteel promenade park that ran between the lanes of Commonwealth Avenue.

Diana and I played around a bit on our bikes, riding at each other like lancers and terrorizing the squirrels. Usually I was content to follow her lead, but that afternoon, I had more than bike play on my mind. So, I hopped off my bike and waited for her to make another pass around. She rode straight at me, trying to hold my gaze with that badass "cut me off and die" riders' glare, but my eyes just slid from the gray lenses of her sunglasses down to her bunched cleavage. Noting my stare, she made it a point to ride in close and over my foot.

When she circled back, she was holding her canister of capsicum, threatening me with a blast of the hot pepper spray. I stood my ground, hoping that she didn't have carbon monoxide narcosis, and drew my water bottle. The standoff ended in a stalemate, even though I was clearly outgunned. Diana clicked out of her pedals, straddled her top tube, and gave me a good sweaty hug.

"Hey, you," she greeted me, panting a bit. "Ready for some lunch?"

I kissed her instead of answering. She was restless in my arms but her lips stayed on mine. Our helmets bonked gently. An aroma of coffee, sweat, and even exhaust began to give way to a heady smell of exertion and urgency. It was a normal spring day, just barely warm, but the two of us were slick with a fresh wash of sweat. I'd moved my hands down from her back and she'd begun moving her hips, rocking the bike she still straddled back and forth. We'd become a little too hot a little too fast for this spot.

I knew a place nearby where we could quit playing around. It should have been a tourist attraction but a fire a few years ago had destroyed the big rose window that made it famous. I told Diana that this time she was going to have to follow me and then grabbed all I could of her, to make sure she'd think it was worth it.

Some days, the city's cathedrals seem like ruins already. Soot and worse coat them like Pompeian ashes; pollution and the traffic's ceaseless rattling powder away the mortar, new fragments fall away to the pavement every day. If you care to look, you'll see the gargoyles now wear halos of nails and barbs, a new layer of menace added to keep the pigeons from nesting. Below, every casement, doorway, and ledge is sealed off with chain-link fencing to ward away the city's refugees.

We rode up the handicap ramp and down a passageway between the buildings. I led Diana over to a corner of the fence that had been folded back. We locked our bikes together and ran a chain and padlock around them to the aluminum fence post. They were in the shadow of a neglected portico and would probably be out of sight. I held the jagged edge of the fence for her and then she for me as we slipped inside. The fence had covered the outside access to a courtyard connecting the cathedral and a small adjoining chapel. Around the perimeter of the courtyard ran a dark covered walkway; the whole area still held some of the wet cold from the winter in its granite stones and appeared to be still closed for winter. Both of us instinctively moved into a shaft of sunlight, standing close together to contain our warmth.

We unclasped our helmets without speaking. The wintry drips of the still-thawing courtyard were louder than the trucks outside. I think the peace felt a little uncomfortable to both of us. Diana was a being of the noise and frenzy of traffic; I'd never known her in this kind of silence. We stood facing each other; I put my hands on her hips and she leveled me a forthright gaze that sent me horripilating.

"You're steaming, you know," she told me. She didn't mean it figuratively. We had so much stored heat between us that we were wrapped in a mist of our own making. I mumbled something dumb about being hot into her throat and she slid her rough gloved hand down the back of my tights. I couldn't help but press against her. Our tongues met and our teeth clicked. I was mashing my chest against her breasts as she drew my groin to hers. I loved the scratch of her padded glove on my ass, but I had to pull her arm away so that I cold lift her courier bag and T-shirt up over her shoulders. The thing weighed at least twenty pounds, even without the locks.

Fraying duct tape and old toe-clip straps attached some of the various tools of her trade to the webbed strap of her courier bag. The weight of that bag pulled the strap taut to her chest, cutting an angle between her breasts and bunching up the ratty sleeveless T-shirt she wore over her heavy black halter. A formidable ring of keys with an attached chrome police whistle hung from her neck on a wire cord. The bag strap held it in close to her body and out of the bike's spokes.

We stood at arm's length. I realized that without her bag, she was only a black sheen of spandex and lycra away from naked. The sides of her eyes were crinkled in a smile; she was looking down to my stomach. Trapped by the elastic fabric of my tights, my cock had grown straight upward to the waistband, clearly outlined and beyond my control. Diana giggled a bit, grabbed it, and pulled me in. That was all I could stand.

I moved my thigh between her legs, put an arm around her back and the other at the nape of her neck. Then I gave her a none-too-graceful dip. I kissed her from her earlobe to her throat and then dragged my teeth along her windpipe to her clavicle. I pulled the neck of her T-shirt and halter strap off her shoulder and followed them with my mouth. Long ago, the courier bag had worn a groove into her collar bone, I could feel the dent with my lips. I bit her lightly there, the bone between my teeth, like a bit. Diana moaned and pulled at my back, pushing her breasts closer to my face.

We began to kneel together. I lowered myself into a genuflection and she straddled my upraised knee, squeezing it with biker's thighs. She moved her hands back to the waistband of my tights, pulling it down so that she could wrap her hand around my cock. I wanted so badly to hold her breasts together and present myself with her nipples. I pushed her shirt and halter up and

over them and caught a red bud with my teeth, chewing
just a little. She gave my cock a squeeze that nearly
tipped us over.

It wasn't until we had nearly tumbled to the floor of
the walkway that I gave a thought to where we were. It
wasn't the first time I'd snuck in here, but I'd always
been alone. I'd never really figured out whether I was
trespassing or not. As long as you look like you've got
someplace else to sleep for the night and look a bit
somber, you can usually linger in a church for as long
as you like. A phrase from long ago drifted into my
head, "inappropriate behavior." That was when Diana
took my cock into her mouth. Praise the Lord, I
thought.

I moved my hand along her spine and down to her
bottom and then ran my fingers along the cleft of her
ass to where I could feel the moist heat of her pussy
through the taut lycra. The clinging fabric was almost
translucent over the round of her bottom, so I pulled it
even tighter to feel the steam and folds swelling between her legs. I drew the shorts' chamois padding
tight against her swelling labia. She shifted her knees
apart and nearly swallowed me, while pushing herself
back into my hand. The lycra of the shorts became an
extension of my glove, frustrating and exciting us as I
explored her with my fingers. Through the slick fabric I
found the hard bead of her clitoris and stretched the
elastic around it. Diana growled low in her throat,
sounding a warning. I felt such an urgency, stroking her
through her shorts. I wanted to rip a slit through the
stretch fabric, to see her glowing and wet in tattered
shorts. I knew that growl, though. This was no time to
rush. I massaged her clitoris, circling it slowly with my

fingertips and scanned the windows facing the courtyard. There were no signs that the church was inhab-
ited, even the saints in the stained glass had their backs
to us. I think Diana had abandoned any thoughts of
decorum back in the park; I knew she'd love coming to
the cathedral, the whole idea that we could sin together
was an arousing novelty.

As if to take command of my wandering thoughts,
she squeezed my cock with both of her hands, forcing
even more blood to its rigid head. Then, with her two
lower front teeth, she scraped an excruciating path from
its engorged cowl all the way down its shaft to the root.
I bucked and my reflexes tried to twist me out of her
grip but the rush of pleasure had locked my muscles.
Once I got my eyes facing forward again, I moved my
hand through Diana's hair and she met my eyes. I
smiled in the goofy way that all men in my position are
doomed to do, and she responded with such a ferocious
look, I thought the Virgin Mary had just called me back.

The two of us rose, my palms covering her nipples,
both of her gloved hands still tightly wrapped around
my shaft. We took a few steps over to a granite bench
against the outside wall. Before we sat, I rolled her
shorts down below her bottom, savoring the slight
bulge of her belly. Each roll of her hem revealed more of
what had probably never been exposed before in that
courtyard. When the band of rolled lycra crossed the
curls of her pubic hair, I was intoxicated.

It was the curls that did it to me. I twined my fingers
in the ringlets; they were slick and matted with her
arousal. She was flushed, her skin was pink from her
forehead to her belly. She looked windburned but she
was radiant like a brazier. I slid my hand over the low-

ered waistband and held the pulsing flesh between her legs. She bent her knees just a bit, parting the lips of her vagina around my fingers; I could smell musk in her breath. We fondled each other just like that for a while, almost staggering, our shirts pulled up and our shorts pulled down, my fingers sunk in her hungry mouth. I'm sure neither of us were planning to lie down on that bench, the granite would just suck the heat straight out of our bodies.

We'd fucked plenty of times, usually just in my apartment, and it had become our custom for her to provide the condom. I'd always admired the economical skill with which she'd produce the little packet and affix it, disallowing for the slightest bit of awkwardness. She performed that trick as we groped in front of the bench; I think she might have had the packet hidden in the back of her glove. Then with the same grace and authority, she turned, grabbed the back of the bench and with her arms outstretched and legs nearly straight she turned to look at me over her shoulder, and snarled, "Come on!"

She reached between her legs, grabbed my penis by its length and used the bulb of its head to rub herself up and down. As she ran it along her vulva, I held back, letting her take my cock in just as far as she liked. She stiffened each time it brushed her clitoris; every time I felt her shudder, my resolve quickened. I had to be in her. I had to feel my hipbones straining against the toned muscles of her buttocks. I moved into her and she welcomed me by squeezing my cock inside of her. Diana and I gasped together.

We must have both looked forward at the same time. Just over the bench she had braced herself against was an alcove containing a small cement statue of a robed saint with outstretched arms. We were blessed; I thrust my cock into her, urging myself to be as thick and as long as I'd ever been. This was where we'd been riding to all day. I held her breasts and she kept her hand between her legs, slamming her pelvic bone against my thighs.

As we found our cadence, her knuckles whitened and her breath grew raspy. I folded my arms around her waist, drawing her arched back into my stomach. She kept her eyes on the weathered saint and smiled like a gutsy pagan. I tangled my face in her hair and my teeth found the back of her neck. She flexed all at once and then began to change the tempo, coming back to meet my thrust with such determined force that I had to step back to brace myself. I looked back to the stained glass. The angels weren't going to be any help now, I couldn't hold back much longer.

"Right now," I told her, putting it as simply as I could. She pounded back into me and began to laugh. It was damn frightening, there in the church. Her throaty, sure, growling joy gathered a new magnitude from the granite arches and domes. For a moment, the statuary and gargoyles joined her in an ululation that must have had my voice in it too. Then I convulsed, my belly slipping on her sweaty back, probably giggling, too.

She'd taken more than I knew I had, and for days afterward I could still smell her on my gloves and in my hair. I could hardly ride home that day, and didn't touch my bike again until the weekend.

IN THE SACRED AND PROFANE COUNTRY OF THE FLESH

Tsaurah Litzky

IN THE SACRED and profane country of flesh the body
does not lie. There is mercy in the body and there are
warnings: Danger, Thin ice, Beware! When I ran across
my kitchen to embrace you on your birthday, you pat-
ted me stiffly on the shoulder and I knew she had won
and the horror of it, I gave her the ammunition, I told
her that you cross-dressed, I didn't know her well
then, I didn't know what she was looking for, I should
have picked up on it when she spoke of her Scottish
lover Ryan, when she said you haven't made love until
you've made love to a man in a kilt, I should have
known right then it was you she was after. Her generous favors to me, her flattery, were all strategies in her
campaign, and even if I prove to you that she manipu-
lated me, even if I take you through it step by step, I

know it will not make any difference to you now, you are her slave, her willing captive, with her tongue she has chained you, with her sex she has tied you down, she has told you she is in your shoes, she has promised you protection, there's nothing I can do and it's all so boring anyhow, it's such an old story, the eternal triangle and I am the rejected lover, beating her breast, wallowing in pain, how trite, how mundane, it's Crisco on the toothbrush, it's moldy white bread, it's a sink of dirty dishes, it's a rat inside my head.

I remember when I started to unravel, I had let myself into your place with the key you gave me, I wanted to surprise you, I wanted you to find me naked in your bed, it was cold in our apartment, I was reading John Cheever under the covers, then I got up and went to your closet looking for a blanket and found instead, under some towels, a big black rubber penis covered with Vaseline. I knew right away it was a dildo though I had never seen one before, it blew me away. I remember how I took it out of the closet, it was still warm, and put it on your kitchen table, I took off my engagement ring and stuck it right on the Vaselined tip and drove weeping home on the expressway, it was a wonder I wasn't killed, you called me on the telephone when you came in, you were frantic, you said you loved me, why should I care what you stuck up your ass, you said you brought the dildo because you wanted to control your urges, you didn't want to go with men anymore, we reconciled, we didn't speak of the dildo incident again, but it was never the same for me after that, I began to find fault with you, to look for weakness, now I wouldn't care if you had a hundred dildos in every color of the rainbow, I wouldn't care if you had a dildo tree, if only we could sit together and drink coffee, take long walks, tell each other stories, if only you still had ears for me.

DEVELOPER

Annie Regrets

THE FIRST TIME I masturbated in the darkroom it took me forty-five minutes, but since then I've modified the procedure somewhat. It's become a ritual, my fixer orgasm. I try to keep it to five to ten minutes, and my goal is efficiency, not eroticism. Afterward, I usually take a little break, grab a Coke out of the darkroom fridge, then sit and feel my genitals gradually lose their heat, receding back into my body to their quiet, dry, everyday place between my legs.

One Saturday night I was, as usual, in the darkroom, developing, printing, and masturbating. This time, after I came, with my tights moist and sticking to my thighs, I went to grab my habitual Coke, but the fridge was empty. I remembered an old vending machine down the corridor on the other side of the basement, so I wad-

dled, squinting, down the brightly lit corridor in search
of hydration.

When I returned and shut the darkroom door behind
me, I couldn't see a damned thing; my eyes had grown
accustomed to the brightly lit hallway. As I went to flick
on the overhead lights, a voice somewhere in front of
me said softly, "No. Please don't."

It was a male voice, unfamiliar to me.

"Why not?" I asked, frozen by the door.

Silence.

"Because," he said, still quietly, "we need to talk."

"We do?" I automatically snapped back. I groped in
the darkness, found a counter, and set the Coke down
gingerly.

"Please promise that you'll hear me out."

"OK." My eyes were beginning to readjust to the
darkroom's red light. But all I could see were nebulous
clusters of amorphous black shapes. "What are you doing here, anyway?"

"Because we need to talk," he repeated. I felt something brush past me to my left. I instinctively reached
out, and felt nothing. Then, there were hands on my
shoulders. He was directly behind me. I sensed his
body, his legs, his chest, very close to mine. He radiated
a warmth that I could feel although he was still inches
away.

His hands remained light on my shoulders. "Don't be
frightened."

But I was.

He began to massage my shoulders and back, and I realized how long it had been since someone else's hands
had touched me, in places my own hands couldn't reach.
I had forgotten how many sensitive areas there are

tucked away on the human body. He was talking, but I was only half-listening, enchanted by his hands on my shoulders and now, lightly caressing the length of my back with a finger. From the bottom of my neck, his finger trailed down my spine until it reached its base, then meandered a lazy path back up to my neck and down again, each trail cutting deeply. The boiler rumbled on the other side of the wall. He didn't say his name.

"Give me your right hand," he demanded suddenly, and I did. He leaned over, pressing the length of his body against mine as he took my hand in his, and then he lifted it to his nose. "I also know how you pass your time down here."

As surprise and anger swiftly rose in me, he brought my hand to his mouth, kissed it and began licking my fingers. He took two fingers inside his warm, wet mouth, closed his lips around them, and slowly withdrew them, lightly sucking, savoring the lingering sweet brine of my pussy.

I was mortified that he had learned my secret darkroom pastime, but in my thick sensual stupor, I couldn't resist him sucking my fingers, stroking my back. I could feel my pussy, still slick from before, begin to throb heavily again. I bent forward slightly, rubbing my ass against his groin, and I could feel, with each movement, his cock growing harder, and my pussy growing wetter.

He removed my hand from his mouth, put his arms around my waist, and pushed his crotch deeply against my ass. His hands worked their way upward, starting at my thighs, moving across my pubis, over my stomach, to my breasts. When his hands found me braless, his cock leaped against my buttocks. His hands deftly rubbed my nipples until I let out a deep moan, and my knees buckled. He lifted me up and turned me around to face him.

He had short, dark, curly hair, and charcoal eyes that reflected the red light of the room. That was all I could make out in the semi-darkness. He smiled at me, then pulled me to his chest and kissed me. We became entangled in hair, smooth, strong lips moist and graceful, tongues tangling and probing, pushing and exploring, and me scratching my soft cheek against his rough, stubbled one.

Then with lips sloppy from kisses and burned cheeks stinging, I pulled away and raised his T-shirt, revealing a strong, wide chest. I kissed the curls of hair between his nipples, then wound my tongue around the nearest nipple, gently pushing my knee into his groin. He moaned and grabbed my buttocks with both hands, lifting up my miniskirt. With an elegant flick, the skirt was off. His hands equally deftly removed my T-shirt, and I wrestled with the buttons on his fly. I gasped as his enormous dick, rigid and thick, sprang free from his trousers, fully erect.

The cotton crotch of my tights was sopping, and he pushed his cock between my legs, rubbing it against my wetness. His cock soon became slick, and he reached down to angle the top against the cotton panel, stroking me into delirium.

He gently eased me down to the cold concrete floor as he tossed off his shirt. Crouching on top of me, sweaty and feverish, he sucked and nibbled the tips of my breasts while my hands frantically searched for and found his cock. I tenderly stroked its head with a finger drenched in my juices; it twitched and shook back at me.

I pressed his body firmly down onto the floor, and as I did I noticed that he held a fresh condom in his hand; I hadn't even seen him take it out. I gently wrested it from him and rolled it slowly down his beautiful hard dick, leaning into him to take his balls in my mouth while I stretched the condom down inch by inch. Once it was firmly in place, I took his balls in my hand and began to nibble on the tip of his cock. He moaned as I eased it deep into my mouth, and shouted when I suddenly shoved the last few inches in and gave him a tremendous upward suck. His sweaty, glistening body, all sinews and dark curls, shook as I licked the exposed base of his dick with my tongue. I moved, straddling his face with my legs, still sucking hard on his cock and fondling his balls.

I heard a *r-r-r-i-ipppp* as he tore away the soaked crotch of my tights, and then began to rub my wet labia with his fingers, back and forth. I twitched and oozed fragrant juice as another finger, wet and slick, massaged my asshole and then entered it, slowly licking its way inside. I threw my pelvis onto his fingers, grinding my pubis against them, and let out a little cry as he wriggled them into my dripping vagina.

He pushed me away and positioned me on all fours, with my ripped tights and ass thrust high in the air. He swiftly yanked down the waistband, spreading my legs from behind. Holding his cock in his hands, he pushed it between my legs and rubbed the head against my slick, elongated clitoris. I was shaking with pleasure as he rubbed his hard cock against me and I screamed when, unexpectedly, he inserted the first several inches of his dick with a slow, deft push. He shook his penis back and forth inside of me, and I slowly inched backward, taking in more of his thick cock with each pelvic grind and wriggle.

He began to fuck me slowly from behind, holding me by the waist and very deliberately withdrawing, pausing, and then deeply plunging inside again. Each time he entered me, my heavy full breasts, pink and ripe from caresses and bites, would sway and I would feel my muscles tightening around his cock. My nipples seemed to brush full against the air, and grow harder with each swing.

When I moved in tandem with him, matching his thrusts with my legs closing around his cock, eager to intensify my pleasure, he would either stop altogether or proceed at a crawl. He would enter so slowly that I could feel every muscle, every ripple and contour of his dick, and then, once firmly inside, would gradually retreat again, leaving me engorged and dripping. He'd gradually increase his thrusts, and I, craving the full force of his cock slamming into me, would put my hands around it and guide it deeper inside, feeling it strain against my vaginal walls. Then his thrusts would stop; he'd lean over and kiss me deeply on the lips, our tongues colliding in a frenzy of spit and flesh, madly probing and searching. My pelvis would rise up, legs akimbo, begging him to enter me again.

When he said, "I want to watch your face when you come," my heart skipped a beat. He softly stroked my cheek; I clasped his hands in mine, and then firmly pressed them to the floor as I twisted and writhed, shaking his cock inside of me. The juice from my pussy drizzled out and caught in his pubic hairs. When I could no longer bear not to come, I moved his cock in-

side me quicker and deeper, his smooth, hard dick in-
flaming my vagina. He bucked his pelvis into mine, his
cock glistening with my juice, sliding in and out, the ex-
plosion of my orgasm gaining intensity with every
slam. I felt his penis throbbing wildly inside of my cunt,
and I felt as if the walls of my vagina were peeling off.

We both came with a tremendous shudder, each of us
tearing at flesh, screaming and panting with pleasure
and release. We clung to one another, there on the darkroom's concrete floor, our musky odors and sweat com-
mingling with those of the stop bath and fixer, softly
glowing in the deep red of the safelight, listening to the
boiler and to the sounds of our own heavy breathing.
My head lay on his heaving chest, his chest hairs matted by perspiration and kisses, and he stroked my hair.
Suddenly, I had this desire for a Coke. I realized that the
one I had fetched was on some counter somewhere,
and I laughed aloud.

ABSOLUTION

Tom Caffrey

ALTHOUGH HE WAS not aware of it, the one he had been waiting for came on the train from Hungary, which pulled into the yard several hours after midnight, its lights cutting through the falling snow and the steam from its brakes rolling along the tracks like the breath of a muttering workhorse. When the guards opened the big wooden doors, the people spilled onto the platform like stones scattered from a child's hand. Disoriented from long hours in the cold without food or water, they stood in frightened groups, the few possessions that had not been taken from them clutched tightly in frozen fingers.

He had been doing his job long enough to know not to linger too long on their faces. It was easier if he was able to think of them as creatures without identities. Even when he read their names from the lists, ordering them into various groups, he did not allow himself to linger on the particulars, did not let his mind attach the words his mouth called out with the shapes that scurried past his vision just out of sight.

He cupped his hands and blew into them, trying to bring warmth to his skin. It was bitterly cold, and he had forgotten his gloves back in his quarters, having excused himself early from the weekly card game in order to attend to the latest arrivals. Thankfully there were only a few hundred in the latest shipment, perhaps a thousand at most. It would take little more than an hour or two to get them all cataloged and sent to the proper buildings. Because of the train's late arrival, weeding out those who would be useful and those who would be eliminated quickly would wait until morning. Once his work was done he could return to the comfort of his bed and sleep late.

He fished the list from his coat pocket and began to call out. One after another, shadows separated themselves from the groups and flitted into the lines he created with a sweep of his finger. Men here and women there, children to stay with the mothers until they could be evaluated for their ability to carry rocks or scrub floors. Occasionally he was aware of a wail as two with the same name were pushed into different lines, one calling out to the other. But the cries rang dully in his ears, muffled by his own voice as he moved quickly down the pages.

When he reached the end of his list he looked up, anticipating the comforting sight of the neatly apportioned groups created by his having done his job correctly. As expected, the aimless throng that had emerged from the train now stood in ordered knots, their faces shrouded in darkness. He smiled to himself, pleased at his work. He motioned for the guards to march them to the appointed units. As they filed silently away into the night, he pulled his collar tight against the snow and turned to walk back to his room.

Then he saw that one remained. Unattached to any of the groups, he stood in a circle of lamplight beside the train, not moving. His hands were stuck deeply into the pockets of his worn coat, his shoes covered by the drifting snow as he waited patiently, surrounded by the pale light.

He walked over to the man, incredulous that any could be left standing. At first he thought that perhaps the man was dead, had somehow frozen while standing still. But as he got closer he saw that the man's breath was frosting the air, escaping from between his lips in small clouds. While still some feet away, he called out to the man, but received no answer. He called again, his voice retreating into the silence as before.

Angered, he rushed forward and struck the man on the side of the head, watching as he crumpled to his knees in the snow. He was preparing to deliver another blow when the man looked up directly into his face. The face was that of a man much the same age as he himself was. The skin was faded with cold, the heavy bones beneath the surface more prominent than they should have been. The eyes were dark, as if there were no end to them, and he could not stop gazing into them. From the cracked lips, a thin line of blood spread downward.

For several moments he stood, his arm raised, unable to move. When he was able to draw himself away, he could not bear to speak to the man, to hear words drop from the bruised mouth. Instead he motioned for a guard to come. Unwilling to touch the man himself, he gave orders for him to be taken to one of the units and then walked quickly away before the chill that had begun to creep into his skin could burrow any deeper inside.

Back in his room he stripped quickly and drew a bath. He sunk into the hot water, letting it close around him like a huge hand, holding him firmly in its welcoming grasp. He shut his eyes and tried to force the encounter with the man from his mind. Several times he succeeded, only to have the face slash the clean fabric of his thoughts like a knife, slicing it to ribbons as the pieces tumbled around him. He scrubbed at his hands until they were raw, trying to banish the touch of the man's flesh from his skin. As he rubbed, he felt again the force of his blow as it connected with the bones of the man's face, watched helplessly as he fell again and again into the snow as the scene repeated itself against the wall of his vision.

Rising from the bath he dried himself, feeling colder than he had before entering the water. Most of all, he was disturbed that he should have even remembered the man's face. Never before had he noticed the recipients of his blows, feeling as his fist struck home that he was simply doing what was required of him. It meant nothing, had no effect outside of that moment in time but to achieve what needed to be done.

As he tried to sleep, the man's face hung above him like a moon, the blood-stained lips inches from his own, the dark eyes unblinking and brilliant as new stars. When he finally drifted into unconsciousness shortly before dawn, his sleep was fitful, broken by the recurring image of himself reaching out to touch the man's face only to have it dissolve into nothingness.

He went about his work the next day with an uncharacteristic listlessness. He avoided contact with the detainees and remained for most of the morning in his office. His lack of enthusiasm was noticed by the other officers, and he invented a story about a stomach ailment to disguise the sense of dread that had germinated within him. When in the afternoon he caught himself staring out the window at a woman working near the drainage ditch, and noticed that her hair was the color of autumn leaves, he left quickly, saying that he was not feeling well and would return in the morning.

That night he drank heavily from a bottle of vodka, each swallow pushing the image of the man deeper into the void created by the numbing alcohol. When the sting of his blow had become a dull ache in the bones of his hand, he began to laugh. With each release of sound, the features of the man's face became more obscured, less clearly defined in his memory until they had taken on the shapeless form that he was used to seeing, one that he could buffet and bend at will until it became a thing that he controlled. Once he saw that the man was in fact no more than any of the rest of them, in fact did not even exist in any real world, he collapsed in waves of triumphant laughter that tapered off until they faded into the ragged breath of sleep.

The next day, still hung over, he was able to walk around the camp shrouded in the familiar veil through which he viewed his daily activities there. He had ventured out tentatively at first, afraid that once again the faces would be in sharp detail, that he would be unable to cover the length of the compound without his carefully constructed armor being pierced by the momentary glimpse of a worker's half-opened mouth or a stray lock of hair escaped from beneath a head covering.

But after walking past several work crews without incident, he began to feel better. The figures that moved about him were once again someone else's irrelevant details, really nothing more than numbers that could be shuffled around to obtain the desired result. If the new total was somewhat less than yesterday's, it was of no real consequence. It made him happy to have overcome the incident with the man, as though he had won some very important battle by erasing the image from his memory.

His confidence remained intact for the entire day as he went about the routine of dispatching new arrivals to the various locations, supervising the shoveling of snow from the walkways, and attending to the various details necessary for making the camp the efficient clearinghouse that it was. He had completely forgotten the man who had shaken him so badly until he looked up during a conversation with one of the furnace operators and saw the man staring at him from behind a fence, his hands grasping the wire as if it were a lifeline.

While the figures around him stayed softly out of focus, the man shone like a bright light in stark detail. His hair had been shorn and he was wearing a faded pair of camp overalls, but the eyes were the same. When he looked into those eyes, his world shattered, the fragments falling through the ever-widening hole in his defenses, leaving him naked and very frightened. He leaned heavily against the wall, and shut his eyes tightly as he tried desperately not to be sick. The man he had been talking to asked him several times if he was all right before he responded, hastily excusing himself and running for the safety of his room.

Falling to the floor, he lay there for several hours, his chest heaving as he sucked in air raggedly and tried to calm the pounding in his head. Night fell and flooded his room with inky darkness, yet he did not move. He was waiting for the world to swallow him up, to take on the form of the man's face as the mouth opened and took him in, grinding his bones between its broken teeth. When nothing happened, he began to cry.

As soon as the morning filtered through the clouds, he began to search for the man. Now he had moments of great clarity, and the visions blinded him. He recoiled as a line of women, their faces sunken and ash-colored, were led past him, the faded patterns of their dresses lashing out to wrap around his throat. When he saw a child, the blue of her stockings startling against the whiteness of her skin, holding her mother's hand as they waited in a line he knew led to death, he had to resist the temptation to snatch her in his arms and run.

Instead, he staggered by hurriedly, frantically looking for the face he could not forget, the one that could end his torment. For the rest of the day he moved among the sea of bodies, hoping that each turn would bring him face to face with the cure he needed so badly, the thing that would end his suffering. But his search turned up nothing, leaving him exhausted and broken as the day burned away into evening and the snow began to fall again.

Lying naked and shivering on his bed, he called to death. He thought that perhaps if he tried hard enough, he could will his heart to cease the rhythmic beating that kept the blood coursing through his veins, that perhaps the cold would wrap its fingers around his nakedness and caress him into oblivion. He thought again of the child he had seen, about the thousands like her whose souls soared over the world in the thick black smoke that swirled from the chimneys he worked so hard to keep in order. He begged her to snatch the life from his chest and hold it in her tiny hands as an offering to whatever god would forgive him what he had done.

The door of his room opened and snow scurried across the floor like frozen moths. The man was standing there, dressed in his ragged overalls, his bare feet buried in the drifting whiteness. He watched as the man walked silently into the room and the door slid quietly shut behind him. The man stood beside his bed now, looking down at him.

Sliding to his knees, he knelt in front of the man, his head bent. Reaching out, he touched the bare feet, feeling beneath his fingers the cold that clung to them like another skin. Leaning down, he touched his lips to the flesh, feeling it stir beneath his kiss as he breathed warmth across the foot. Looking up, he gazed again into the eyes that had shown him more than he could bear to see, had unlocked the gates to a world of which he was a creator but which he had never visited until these last few days.

The man unbuttoned his overalls and slid them from his shoulders, letting them fall to the floor. He caught them in his hands, feeling the thinness of the material on his skin, seeing for the first time the stark yellowness of the star that had been sewn on the left-hand side directly over the heart. The man stepped out of the overalls and he slid them to one side. Now both were naked, the one standing above the other.

He looked up at the man's body, thin with hunger and pain. He felt the hair on the chest and legs, so different from his own smooth skin. It was this and the many other differences between them that had allowed him to hate, that had allowed him to laugh as the black smoke choked the sky and the ash fell like rain on the camp.

He looked too at the man's cock. Long and thin, its head hung down naked and round, the nest of skin that capped his own prick missing. He took the end between his lips, his tongue sliding over the soft ball of flesh as it sank into his mouth. He closed his eyes, letting the man's prick fill him. As he sucked gently on it, the shaft began to swell with heat. He was surprised at how large the man was, at how thick his cock had become.

He worked his mouth along the length of the fully erect prick, his lips sliding over the silky skin as he urged the man further into his throat. The thick head pushed along his gullet, choking him at the same time that it filled him with pleasure. The man's skin tasted of sweat, and he washed it carefully with his tongue, licking every inch as it passed over his lips, sucking from him the film of grime.

His hands were on the man's asscheeks, pushing him against his face. The flesh beneath his hands was rough with hair, the bones pressing into his palms where he grasped the man tightly. As he sucked his dick, the man began to thrust slowly in and out, fucking his face steadily. As the cock slipped past his lips, it became slick with spit. Soon a steady stream was dripping from the man's balls, falling onto his feet in small drops. The man had placed his hands on his head, as though to bless him, and he could feel the thin fingers entwined in his hair as he moved up and down the huge prick between his lips.

He felt the man's touch on his shoulder and stopped sucking. Pulling himself up, he lay on his back on the bed. His own cock was hanging heavily between his legs, his balls begging him to attend to them. But he knew that this night had nothing to do with his pleasure, and he left them untouched.

The man knelt between his thighs and pulled his legs up over his shoulders. He felt the tip of the big cock against his asshole. As the man shoved into him, he cried out in pain. The thick shaft tore at his insides, sending fingers of pain clawing through his belly. But inch after inch poured into him, not stopping until he felt the man's thick bush against his ass.

The man began to fuck him, retreating and entering in long motions, his balls slapping against his butt as he pumped, the fingers biting into his skin where they held his thighs. His legs slid over the bones of the man's chest as they moved together, his flesh scraping against the hair. The man thrust harder, forcing his cock deep into his asshole, pulling almost all of the way out before sinking in again.

He looked up at him and remembered the first time he had seen that face. Although shorn of his hair, the man's face still reflected the look of knowing that had roused such anger in him that night. The dark eyes remained clear and bright, even as he plowed into the tender ass beneath him. The man pulled out and began to beat his cock with his hand. After a few strokes he came, the thick drops flying from his prick and raining down, falling over his face and onto his chest. He tasted the spunk on his lips, felt it tangled in his hair and running sweetly down his neck.

He began to weep, burying his face in his hands. The man bent down and gently pried his fingers open, holding his hands in his own. Then he kissed him softly, the cracked lips covering his for a moment. Opening his eyes, he saw that the man's mouth was set in a small smile, the corners of his lips upturned. Then, without a word, the man turned and walked out the door naked into the snow.

He slept that night covered in the sticky remains of the man's come, his sleep uninterrupted save for a dream in which a child in blue stockings held out her arms to him and he lifted her up as she laughed with a voice like rain.

MARIAN'S EARS

Susan St. Aubin

WHEN JOE TURNER came into Hal's office cubicle and started complaining about his ears, Hal could only see Marian's ears, small and pink as shells, slightly peaked at the top like elf's ears, a very different organ from Joe's fleshy, hairy protuberances. Joe stuck his little finger in one ear and wiggled it around.

"Plugged," he said, "completely plugged. What do you think?"

Hal thought of Marian's pink shells. "See a doctor," he suggested, shrugging at his computer screen while he scrolled up a menu. Joe melted out of his vision into the next cubicle, his voice fading to a mutter.

Marian was the only woman Hal knew who still had unpierced ears. Even his mother had had gold studs nailed through her earlobes in a department store one Saturday afternoon. His wife, Evelyn, had three holes in each ear, two in each lobe and one on each side, where she wore two gold rings that stuck out at angles from her head.

Hal first discovered the secret of Marian's ears when he touched them after dinner one Sunday while they were sitting at the card table at the foot of her bed in the center of her one-room apartment. He reached both arms across the table and gently stroked down from their peaked tips to their small lobes, connected to her jaw instead of hanging loose like most people's did.

She shivered, her hands flying up as though she wanted to push him away, but she stopped and breathed deeply as he moved his fingertips across the lobes onto her cheeks. He'd never seen such a reaction, and started to move his fingers back to her ears again.

"No," she said, putting her hands on his.

Later, in bed, physiology was turned upside down. Instead of reaching between her legs, his fingers went for her ears. She reached up, turned off the lamp beside the bed, and let him stroke the rims, the nearly fleshless lobes, the delicate peaks at the tips. With his tongue he explored one ear's orifice, trying to remember names for the inner convolutions. Labyrinth. Cochlea. Coiled shells.

Marian moaned beneath him, her pulsing ears warm. He bet himself they were red, the way they were when he embarrassed her or made her laugh. When he turned on the light, she sat up, crying out "No" as her hands jumped to her ears.

"You know I don't like the light on!" Her face was flushed. When he took her hands away from her ears, her hair fell over them. She was panting and her forehead was sweaty. He brushed her hair aside but her quick hands were on those ears before he could see a thing, so he kissed her on the mouth, turned off the light, and pulled her back down on the bed. She sighed as he traced the outer rim of her right ear, this time with his tongue, circling slowly into the labyrinth while his fingers stroked her other ear. Her breathing became deeper and faster in time with the rhythm of his tongue and fingers. He put a little finger in each of her ears, tickling the invisible hairs there until Marian gasped and shuddered, then sobbed, "Don't ever tell anyone this, I couldn't bear to have people know."

He paused. "Know what?" he asked, as though he hadn't noticed a thing.

At work he hid medical books about ears in his desk, furtively taking them out when no one was looking. Earlobes have few nerve endings, he read. That's why doctors take blood samples from children's ears, because they won't feel it. Ha, he thought, like baby boys don't feel a thing when their foreskins are peeled off. But when he touched his own ears, he found them strangely numb compared to his face.

She's a secret pervert, he thought. That's why this cool and doll-like girl excites me. Everyone's got some strange sexual button, and I've found hers.

At home in bed with Evelyn, Hal read about ears while she studied the books on French cooking the head chef at Chouette, whose apprentice she was, had recommended. She licked her lips as she turned the pages, but those full, pink lips had temporarily lost their charm for him. He turned back to his own book and read that there are many myths about ears. Wrinkled earlobes, for example, have long been thought to indicate problems in the heart or circulatory system, but, of course, wrinkling of the skin is as common in old age as various heart problems.

Hal reached up to finger his earlobes, which felt perfectly smooth. Even though, as his book said, cause and effect cannot be presumed, he thought he'd take a closer look in the mirror sometime when Evelyn wasn't around to laugh at him. Connected lobes, he read, are a recessive trait in which the lobes, like Marian's, meet the jaw instead of hanging loose. He wondered if ear orgasms could be a recessive predilection, but there was no mention of sex.

He planned his next date with Marian on Friday. Evelyn worked at Chouette mostly on the weekends: Fridays, Saturdays, and Sundays were the big days; they were closed on Mondays and Tuesdays. Evelyn sometimes spent Friday night with her sister, who lived a block away from the restaurant. It gave them a chance to get caught up, she said. He reached over and stroked Evelyn's earlobe. Without all her rings, her ears looked delicate and damaged, slightly bruised around the holes. He wondered how much it hurt to have the holes done, if even now it was ever painful to wear earrings.

Evelyn dropped her book and lay back with her eyes closed. He continued stroking, his smallest finger moving slowly to the secret and unseen part of her ear. He was more aroused than Evelyn, who breathed lightly, as though asleep. She moved one hand across his thigh to his hardening penis, while her other hand moved his fingers from her ear to her breast.

"Don't you like that?" he whispered.

"Like what?"

He flicked his tongue into her ear and whispered,

"cochlea," loving the sound of the word and the sensation of entrapment that whispering it gave his tongue.

Evelyn laughed. "That tickles! What are you doing?"

"Some people's ears are very sensitive," he said.

He wanted to tell her. There was no reason why he shouldn't; they'd both had lovers before, but unimportant lovers they could laugh about together, like her friend George from New York with his pierced left nipple who tried to talk her into piercing her right nipple so they'd be mirror images. Hal was afraid that if Marian wasn't his secret, he'd be in danger of losing her. Evelyn's laugh could sometimes kill like a frost; she would be capable of making him think Marian's mysterious ears were silly.

She kissed him on the mouth, then slid her mouth down his body to kiss him where Marian never would. "I guess everyone's different," she murmured as her lips sucked his cock into the labyrinth of her mouth. He thought how the human body, especially the female body, was a series of labyrinths tunneling to an unknown center.

The next day at noon, he walked six blocks to the school where Marian taught and stood behind a tree just outside the chain-link fence. In dark glasses, with the collar of his jacket turned up, he watched her play a circle game with a group of children. They all moved right, then left, singing a song whose words he couldn't catch because their voices were so high-pitched. One of the first signs of aging, he remembered, was a loss of hearing at higher frequencies.

Marian's hair covered her ears except when the wind blew it back to reveal their tips, glowing red with the cold. He pulled his face further back into his collar, enjoying the role of voyeur. Once she looked in his direction but didn't seem to recognize him. Surely someone will call the police, he thought. Maybe Marian will when she goes back inside. A squad car will pull up and take me away at Marian's command. His heart beat faster. When no one came to get him after she took her class inside, he went back to work feeling light-headed with freedom. On his way into the office, he bought a bag of pork rinds from a machine in the lobby and ate them as he rode up the escalator.

Friday morning Evelyn kissed him, saying she'd be back early the next day.

"Early enough to get back in bed, if you're there," she whispered.

"I will be," he answered, glad he wouldn't miss Evelyn's Saturday morning seduction, glad Marian didn't like him to spend the night because she was afraid someone might see him leave in the morning—a neighbor or even her landlady.

Hal thought surely one of those watchful people would notice how the lights always went off for hours when he visited, even though no one left the apartment. He and Evelyn would laugh together about something like that, but when he mentioned it to Marian in an attempt to get her to leave just one light on, she didn't understand.

"We could be doing all sorts of things in the dark. We could be watching television in the dark. Having the lights on doesn't mean anything because you always want to do it with the lights on." She reached across him to switch off the lamp on his side of the bed.

Evelyn always liked the lights on and so did Hal because he wanted to see her vaginal lips turn a dark lipstick pink, her breasts rise and tighten and her face flush as dark pink as those inner lips when she came. Even though there was something exciting about scuffling around in the dark, he often wondered what Marian looked like in her secret inner parts, beyond the quick flash of pink lips and lavender interior before she pulled her legs together on the rare times they made love in daylight. There was more to life than ears, he thought.

Friday night after work he climbed the stairs to Marian's apartment, an image of her ears before him. Through the window he could see across the room into the former closet that was her kitchen. Everything seemed to be on a child's scale: miniature gas stove, sink, and counter, with cabinets packed beneath and above. An uncurtained square of window was in the center of the upper cupboards. She was grating cheese, her ears hidden by her hair, which was pulled over them in two loose pigtails. When she came to the door he lifted one to kiss the ear beneath it, but she ducked away and went back to the counter where she was arranging lasagna noodles in a baking dish between layers of cheese and sauce, like weaving a basket, he thought.

"I'm sure Evelyn makes this much better," she said. "I just use my mother's old recipe; it's probably not even really the way Italians do it."

"Evelyn doesn't cook Italian so far," he assured her. "Only French."

While her hands were occupied he pulled the ribbon holding one pigtail, then the other, loosening the silky light brown hair and smoothing it behind her ears in her usual style.

"No," she said, pulling her hair back over her pure, unadorned ears. "Not yet. Wait."

While the lasagna baked they sat side by side on her bed, his arm around her shoulders. They listened to the soft, unidentifiable music she liked, which, when he asked, always turned out to be something like Japanese flute concertos, or instrumental whale songs, or wind chimes played by musicians he'd never heard of. When he brought tapes of Talking Heads or Elvis Costello, she'd listen for a few minutes, then cover her ears.

Once she said, "This isn't very relaxing, is it?"

"Relaxation isn't the point," he answered, but when she looked blankly at him, he realized that, for her, it was.

He leaned his head on her shoulder, sniffing her ear through her hair, getting his nose right inside the vestibule, smelling a scent like dying roses, like rain, like dust. She pushed him away to go check the lasagna.

While they ate, she kept smoothing her hair over her ears with her free hand. Hal thought her hair looked like a helmet pulled down like that, or a nun's wimple. Later, in the dark, he hoped to penetrate that wall of silky hair to free Marian's ears.

"No," she hissed as his fingers felt for her ears. "It's too much, I can't take that much."

"That much what?" he asked.

She mumbled something that sounded like "pleasure."

"What?" he whispered. "What?"

"Nothing," she said. She guided his hand between her legs to her less certain arena of pleasure. He stroked and stroked with his fingers, then entered her, stroking from deep inside, and had his orgasm because he couldn't wait forever for something like that electric reaction she'd had when he touched her ears. He kept trying to sneak his fingers up to them to see what that zap would feel like inside her, but she kept pushing his hands away.

Late at night, walking down the stairs, he watched the clear, cold stars in the wet sea of the sky and thought, she'll stay the same, always hanging like that at the brink of the universe. It'll never be more than this. He sighed as he unlocked his car door, glad he still had Evelyn, his earthly love.

"Did you ever think of piercing your ears?" Hal asked Marian one winter afternoon when they were hiking. She stopped suddenly on the trail as though she'd seen a snake.

"Pierce?" she asked, turning around to face him. Her ears were hidden under the two navy blue mounds of her earmuffs.

"People do that." He laughed at her.

"I don't usually wear jewelry," she sniffed as she walked quickly on ahead.

They came to a meadow with new green grass already poking up beneath the dead grass of last summer. It was almost warm in the sun. They sat facing each other on two large rocks, their hands on their knees.

These hikes were a Sunday afternoon ritual because Evelyn was usually at Chouette from ten in the morning until midnight, doing brunch and dinner. He put his hand on Marian's knees while she looked at a distant ridge through her binoculars, then reached up and slowly removed her earmuffs. Her hair dropped over her ears as she lowered her binoculars to stare at him, the irises of her eyes quickly narrowing in the light.

"Not here," she whispered, turning and raising the binoculars to her eyes again.

"Where?" he whispered. "When?"

She pretended not to hear him.

Back at her apartment she made a vegetable soup, nervously consulting a book called *101 Quick Recipes* that looked old enough to have belonged to her mother. As Hal lay on the bed and watched her work, he imagined these were the simple recipes she was raised on, a contrast to Evelyn's mastery of thousands of sauces and ways to perform fellatio, none of them easy.

Marian frowned. "I'll bet Evelyn would never use *canned* stock," she said, adding chopped carrots, celery, and turnips, and then a can of tomatoes. She crushed dried basil and oregano between her fingers. He loved the smell of herbs on Evelyn's hands when she came home from Chouette, some as simple as sage or tarragon, and others he couldn't identify, not even when she named them.

"Fennel?" he'd ask. "Chervil?"

Marian washed her hands, drying them on a kitchen towel so immaculate it looked new, though he'd seen it often in the past year hanging beside her sink.

"Your soup smells wonderful. Come sit down here while it cooks." When she crossed the room, he took her hands and sniffed the rose scent of her soap, then tried to pull her down to the bed, but she leaned toward the pot on the stove.

"It doesn't have meat in it," she apologized.

When he finally managed to pull her down beside him, she sat stiffly, smoothing back her hair with one hand, while he held the other.

"I don't eat meat half the time," he said. "Evelyn's studying eggs now, so we eat a lot of soufflés, and casserole things with cheese and vegetables. I don't miss meat."

He was staring ravenously at the ears that held back her hair. He was touched she'd bared her ears for him; he thought of telling her he missed them more than meat, but knew she wouldn't understand. He pulled her closer and circled the rims of her ears with his fingers. When she let her eyes shut, he watched the lids pulse and flicker with her breathing. He lowered his tongue to one ear, nudging aside his own finger, thinking she'd never notice the difference, but she opened her eyes at once.

"The soup! It's boiling, it's not supposed to boil!" She shot off the bed to turn it down.

The soup was done. "Overdone," she moaned as she ladled it into bowls.

Hal rolled off the bed to sit opposite Marian at the card table. For him the soup was perfect: the vegetables and noodles well done but not soggy, the broth clear. He even thought Evelyn might approve because she had an appreciation for simplicity as well as variety. He'd seen her open cans. He told Marian the soup was good, but lack of perfection made her sullen. She sipped, frowning, ignoring his slurps and murmurs of appreciation, so soon he was quiet, too.

She got up to put on a tape, something with flutes, and then sat down again. When a noodle, curled like an ear, floated to the surface of his broth, he sucked it up silently from his spoon, letting it slide around his tongue before he chewed and swallowed.

After dinner Marian did the dishes while he drowsed on the bed, listening to the flutes. When Evelyn cooked he did the dishes because she told him chefs were above that, a division of labor that seemed fair to him. He usually did them early in the morning while he listened to the birds at the feeder just outside the window. He realized those flutes carrying on above the clink of the dishes in Marian's miniature sink were someone's idea of bird calls. All wrong, of course; real birds were never that melodiously annoying.

He opened his eyes when he heard the water gurgle out of the sink. Marian dried her hands, then moved through the room turning off lights until she stood beside him.

"Are you asleep?" she asked.

He could see her by the light of the winter moon shining through the high window of her closet kitchen. Her head was bent; the hair fell forward, occluding her ears. She sat on the bed beside him. He reached behind her hair to massage the rims of her ears.

"I have to ask you something," she whispered in his ear while moving his hands off hers. "I have to tell you your obsession with ears bothers me."

"My obsession?"

She lay on her back, arranging her hair over her ears. "It's not normal," she said.

"They're your ears," he answered, "so if you want to call them abnormal that's fine with me."

"It's not my ears," she said, "it's you, always touching them. If you'd just leave them alone, I'd be fine."

"But you like it." He sat up and turned on the light. "I can tell how much you like it. You *come* when I touch your ears."

"I do not." She sat up, her face pink.

He grabbed her hair to hold it off her glowing ears. "Ah hah! See these ears?"

"Hal, please! Turn out the light."

In the moonlight he pulled off her clothes, then stroked her breasts and belly down to her clit, which he took in his mouth and sucked like a nipple while one finger stroked inside her, feeling distant pulsations get stronger. The instant when he knew she'd say, as she often did, that's enough, I've had enough, he lifted his free hand to her ear, stroking from rim to lobe until she rocked beneath him like a boat on a rough ocean, waves lapping and pushing against the finger he still held inside her.

"No, oh, no!" she cried, then lay very still. "Why do you keep doing that with my ears?"

"It's sex," he answered. "I thought you'd like it, I thought that's what we were doing here."

"I don't like it like this," she said. "I don't like to go that far."

When he turned on the light her face was still as pink and swollen as he was sure her inner parts were, as well as her ears, now covered by her damp hair.

"I personally like going as far as I can." He was beginning to feel like a perverted missionary of sex, trying to explain himself to the unheathen. Right now he wanted to be in bed with Evelyn, on the road to eternity, holding her vibrator inside her and nibbling gently at her thighs just the way she wasn't afraid to tell him she liked. Evelyn's way was more ordinary, not quite the challenge Marian presented.

"Maybe I'm just not ready," Marian said.

"Ready for what?"

"I don't know. Men. A lover."

"Ears?" he asked. "You mean you're not ready for ears?"

"I don't see what ears have to do with anything," she said, covering hers with her hands.

He looked at her closely, but she wasn't laughing or lying.

"I guess it's your bad luck you met a man who appreciates ears."

His sarcasm went over her.

"I can't see being into just one thing, that's all," she said. "It's so narrow. What about my legs, my breasts, the things most men like? Why are you so exclusive? When I make love I want all my body parts included, and my mind. All of me."

He stopped listening and kissed her nose, her lips, her fingertips.

"That's nice," she murmured. "You can be so nice."

He was glad to get home to Evelyn, who was sitting up in bed reading a book on Asian cooking. She wore a black cotton gown with cut out embroidered places all around the low neckline. He could see her flesh moving as she breathed.

"Branching out?" he asked. She never could stick to one thing for long; France to Vietnam seemed like a natural culinary progression.

She looked up. "Have you eaten? I brought back some spinach quiche if you want it."

"I ate." He stretched out on the bed beside her.

She returned her attention to her book, but stroked

his hair with one hand until he was nearly asleep.

"Get under the covers," she whispered. She was wearing nothing now, the black gown in a heap beside the bed. He took her breasts in both hands as she kissed him and climbed on top. He liked being seduced for a change. She fit his cock into herself like a cork and began to ride him. His thumbs found her clit, pressing the way he knew she liked. She squeezed his earlobes between her fingers to match his rhythm. This was a sensation he scarcely noticed, like a fly buzzing. He grabbed her around the waist to pull her down harder while he rose up, coming. Every nerve in both their bodies centered between their legs in sparkling points of electricity. Evelyn fell forward on him, her hands on his senseless ears.

Next morning he lifted one of his medical texts to read in bed, carefully so he wouldn't wake Evelyn. In the dim light behind the shades, he read that there may be some truth to the old wives' tale that wrinkled earlobes mean a person is likely to develop heart trouble, because wrinkling of the skin in the extremities can be a sign of poor circulation. A weakening heart doesn't pump enough blood, so the skin withers.

He slid out of bed to go to the bathroom, leaving the open book on his pillow. In the mirror he inspected his ears: the lobes were large, fleshy, and wrinkled, especially the right ear, the side he slept on. When he turned on the light to have a closer look, he discovered even more lines. His ears were criss-crossed with white and red lines. He massaged his right lobe to improve the circulation, but when he dropped his hand his ear was still wrinkled. He thought of Marian's small, smooth, nearly

BEST AMERICAN EROTICA 1995

fleshless lobes, and his heart lurched against his ribs. Was there anything at all to her except ears? He really couldn't see the rest of Marian in his mind. She was right: He was obsessed.

When he came back into the bedroom, Evelyn was paging through his book. She looked up, yawning, and asked, "So, are ears the doorway to the soul? The cochlear passage to the northwest corners of the heart?"

He sat down on the bed beside her.

"Well," he said, "I just noticed my ears are wrinkled. They say that might be an early sign of heart failure."

She laughed, turning the pages of the book. "Where? Where does it say anything like that? Anyway, you're thirty-five, so it should be normal to have a few wrinkles. Look—there's one at the corner of your mouth now. And look at your forehead."

She sat up and pointed. He slapped his forehead with mock horror. Soon they were both laughing.

"They're all bullshit anyway, those medical books," she told him. "What could ears possibly mean? Ears are nothing."

Evelyn could only say that because she didn't know Marian, and if Hal had his way, she never would. He was a man who could tell his girlfriend all about his wonderful wife, to whom he could say nothing about that girlfriend for fear of his own confusion. As he laughed harder he suspected that straight through to his weakening heart and his immortal soul, he was as insensitive as his ears.

FOR LOVE OR MONEY

Mary Malmros

SHE WAS A debt slave, of course. That was all I got anymore. I stared at the new duty roster, angrily checking my assignment against that of the other trainers. Screwed again. I thought about complaining to Mal and quickly rejected the idea. She'd sigh and roll her eyes and subject me to a dreary monologue on how swamped she was with requests for debt-slave training. We both knew there was plenty of call for custom work and chosen-slave training; the roster showed that. But if I brought that up, Mal would change tactics and tell me how I was simply the best in the business for training a debt slave. She thought she was stroking my ego when she spoke like that. In fact, it only made me more angry. My reward for competence at a job nobody wanted to do was more of the same damned job!

I headed for the office, intending to pick up the new

trainee's file and be gone before Mal could see me. She always used paper files, in old-fashioned manila envelopes. She's silly and archaic in some ways. The file was waiting in the outer office, but so was Mal. "Shum, I'm glad to see you," she said warmly. "Did you have a good weekend?"

"It was all right," I said evasively. Mal tends to pry into my personal life a bit. I guess she feels entitled because we were lovers once, years ago, before she decided she preferred men. "Excuse me, Mal, I need to get the file on my new trainee—"

"Ah, yes, I wanted to talk to you about that, Shum." Her expression shifted to one of apology. "I know it's another debt slave, and I feel bad about giving her to you since you haven't had a break in a while, and I know you wanted to try some other things. But really, you're the only trainer that I've got who can do this job."

Her excuses broke down my resolve to avoid an argument. I exploded. "Goddammit, Mal, every time it's the same thing! I deserve better than this and you know it!"

"Better than what? This is a good assignment, Shum. It's a life contract."

I paused in mid-tirade. "Really?"

"Mmm-hmm. The bank just had the claim awarded, and it's a big one. They want a good price out of her. I'm counting on you, Shum. I know you'll do work that's worthy of this House."

She looked so solemn, like an owl. "I'll do my best, Mal," I said soberly, then left the office in haste. I paused halfway down the hall and had a silent, tear-streaked gigglefit in an alcove, then proceeded to the viewing room, my mood considerably improved.

• • •

I found a vacant monitor in the viewing room and sat down, typed in the cubicle number—17—and took a good look at my new trainee.

She was sitting on her bed, back against the wall, forearms propped on her knees. She was naked. All trainees were. For some of them, nakedness would be their default condition during their term of service. She fit the standard mold for a slave: young, reasonably attractive, healthy looking. The only remarkable feature was her medium-length hair. On the monitor, it looked like it would be midnight-dark.

I watched her through the camera, trying to guess what she'd be like. Everybody ran up debts—it was part of the way we lived—but certain types just couldn't handle it. They were the ones who came into my hands. Part of my job was to weed out the ones who weren't fit for slavery and couldn't be trained to it.

The woman on the monitor hadn't moved. I pressed the call button for the handlers' room. Rodney's voice came on the intercom and informed me that training room five was free. He asked me if I had any special instructions. "No, just let me know if she gives you trouble," I said. I was fairly sure she wouldn't.

She was standing in the center of the room when I walked in. I walked over to her, watching her glance flicker between my face and the quirt I held in my right hand.

I spoke. "Kneel."

There were two possible reactions: a futile, "fuck you" defiance, or confused obedience. I watched her face as she digested the command and decided to obey, and then wavered in uncertainty as she thought, as they all did, about how to do it gracefully. She didn't do a half-bad job of it, for a first attempt. We could work on that.

I looked down at her. "Your name is Celin?"

She nodded. "Yes."

"My name is Shum. You will address me as Master." I've never agreed with the use of the term "Mistress" as a generic appellation for all female dominants. It is not, after all, simply a feminine form of "Master." "Mistress" has its own usage, its own connotations. As well, there are meanings in the word "Master" that worked better, at least for me. "I'm going to train you for your new position."

She stared at the quirt. "My new position? What is that?"

"You're a slave. Your duty is to please your master. If you think there are limits to that, think again. If you think it's limited to pleasing your master in bed, by all means think again."

She blushed. "I'm not to be sold . . . for that?"

I made my voice mocking. "Yes, you're to be sold 'for that,' or for any other use that your master wishes. Not many will want to pay the kind of money they'll be paying for you and not use you for sex. You'll scrub floors. You'll polish boots. You'll cook meals. And yes, you'll serve in bed, too."

She nodded slowly. "And you'll teach me?"

The quirt moved much faster than she could react. She fell sidewise, stunned, one hand clutching the side of her face.

"How do you address me?" I said softly.

"Master. I'm sorry, Master," she stammered.

"That's better, slave. Yes, I'll teach you. The first and most important lesson is obedience." I paused, wondering how I could ever properly explain that concept to this irresponsible child. "You know what the word means; you just haven't done much of it. Later, you'll learn to do what you're not told to do, but what your master wants you to do anyway. But that's an advanced topic. For now, you just do what you're told. Understand?"

She swallowed, rubbing the rising welt. "Yes . . . Master," she added hastily, seeing the quirt twitch.

We worked on positions that day, and other areas of basic etiquette. I taught her to drop gracefully to her knees and to rise again, with equal grace. I taught her to walk, to turn, to be aware of herself and yet unaware. I didn't use the quirt again, merely my voice, watching closely to see how she responded. She did reasonably well, but I found myself looking at my watch constantly, bored half out of my mind. If I worked hard, I thought, I might be rid of her in a month or so. But I had to cut the session short. I was just getting more and more depressed and impatient. I called for Rodney to return her to her room; but without even waiting for him to show up, I left her kneeling and confused.

Once at home, I poured myself a glass of mineral water and went to sit on my couch. It's the most expensive piece of furniture I ever bought; it cost me considerably more than my bed, which my infrequent overnight guests have likened to a pallet of cinderblocks covered with tissue paper. I don't even notice that when I sleep. It's when I'm awake that I want comfort, and for that I want my well-padded, leather-upholstered couch. It sits in an alcove in my apartment where I've got a large bay window and a nice west view. It's where I spend most of my time, when I'm not working or sleeping.

I sat and gazed out my window at the sunset, made brilliant by the soot in the air, and tried to think of when my pleasure in my work had turned to dislike. Once upon a time, this had been my dream job. The arguments in favor of accepting full-time employment were persuasive—benefits, a health plan, regular income. "And just think," Mal had said as I'd signed my contract, "you won't have to work at anything else!"

But it was just a job after all, and right now "anything else" sounded pretty attractive. I wanted to move on, but my freelancing skills were rusty. "I take the king's silver and I fight the king's war," I commented aloud. Then, taking another drink of mineral water and wishing it were something stronger, I added, "And I train the king's fucking slaves. Fucking debt slaves."

Mal was one of those who'd set up this system. She was actually proud of it. She boasted about how she'd approached a bank and offered them a novel solution for collecting a student loan that would have taken them twenty years to settle. She'd rigged it, of course. The debtor was known to her, had been in the scene for years, and was an experienced submissive. Mal hadn't had to do much of a sell job to get him to agree. The bank's officers were shocked, at first, but they couldn't find anything illegal about it—it was just a contract, after all—and when the young man in question affirmed steadily that he found the solution acceptable, they reluctantly went along with it. The master and slave were both satisfied with the arrangement, the bank recovered its money in four years instead of twenty, and the industry was born.

Custom work was generally the easiest. While I felt a certain contempt for any would-be master who was unwilling to undertake her own slave's training, it was hard to complain about the work that came to me as a result. The slave, who had already been through the basic course, was generally eager to please and anxious to learn. He or she would be educated in certain skills, taught to anticipate certain idiosyncrasies . . . taught, if possible, to enjoy what would be required. But custom work had rapidly become the province of so-called specialists, such as Jerrold, who could (and would) hold forth for hours on the joys of anal fisting. He was truly a master, but I thought of most specialists as one-trick ponies.

My favorites, of course, are the chosen slaves. I think of them as the true slaves. They seek to learn a higher level of service, not to erase a debt, but to find their proper place. So touching, they are, so hardworking and willing to please. But they're so few, and they all get assigned to other trainers.

My friend and sometime lover Fan does not agree with me. During our most recent (and I hope our last) conversation on this topic, Fan said, "You know what your problem is, Shum? You've forgotten what it's really like, training the 'chosen slaves.' Yes, they're there of their own free will, but they still don't want to be slaves. Not really. They've got their own ideas about what they're after, and their masters have different ideas altogether, and they both call it a master/slave interaction, and they're both wrong. The ones you train are truly going to be slaves. They can't simply back out of it when things don't go the way they wish. They're the only ones that can be taken all the way to their full potential. And you're doing nothing with them, Shum! Nothing!"

The sun dropped lower, and the windows polarized to compensate. It was quitting time for all the people with normal jobs. I watched them milling in the streets below, surging into the subways and over the bridges. "I hate my job!" I yelled down at them. "Do you hate your job as much as I hate mine? I HATE MY JOB!!"

Day two. A day for simple concepts. "Maria. Come here."

Her eyes were cautious. She was learning to think before she reacted. "Celin, Master, my name's Celin," she said softly.

"Wrong. Your name's whatever I choose to name you."

I could see her pause mentally to absorb that. "I understand, Master."

She didn't understand, not yet, but she accepted, and that was enough.

Touch was an issue. It usually was. Some slaves wouldn't stand for it at all. They'd struggle constantly, and have to be broken to it. Some trainers enjoyed doing this brutally. I found that approach counterproductive. The only way to get it over with quickly was to forget about being "quick" and do it right.

I stroked her, and watched as she controlled herself. I understood what she was feeling, what she was afraid of. I knew dozens of tricks to make this easier. Paradoxically, it was usually easier to get them to accept harsh contact rather than a gentle touch. She flinched as my hand grazed her short ribs. I paused. "Are you ticklish?"

"A little bit, Master. Right . . . there," she said, as I found the spot again.

I focused on the spot. "I see." She struggled in vain for control, and I watched, amused, as she began to thrash. Then, relenting, I increased the pressure of my digging fingers until the sensation crossed clearly over the line into pain. The look of relief on her face was almost comical.

I laughed aloud. "Everything's relative, isn't it?"

Her confused look made me laugh more. I stood, with a final pat. "Your skin's dry, slave. Have Rodney give you some moisturizer."

"Yes, Master." She tried to rise from the table and kneel quickly as I left the room, but I didn't wait for her. She'd just have to learn to move faster.

On day five, I decided it was time for her first beating.

"Master? May I ask a question?" she whispered.

She was learning. Pleased, I said, "You may, slave."

"Master . . . why are you beating me? Did I do something wrong?"

She was lying on the table in the training room, where I'd told her to lie. I caressed her back, idly. "No. You haven't done anything wrong. I'm beating you because it pleases me."

She was confused. "Because I did something wrong?" she repeated.

"No. It gives me pleasure. You don't need to understand the wiring, slave. Just deal with it as a black box. You don't need to understand why it pleases me; just accept that it does."

"So . . . when I . . . when I let you—" She hesitated, sensing that the word was wrong, but not knowing the correct one.

"When you submit."

"When I submit to your beating, that pleases you."

"Yes." I smiled.

"That pleases you," she repeated to herself. It sounded trivial, but I knew it was a revelation for her. "Master? Will it hurt?"

"Yes." I smiled, stroking the quirt, watching as she shivered and closed her eyes. "Oh yes."

I'd had the quirt since I was fourteen. I had made it myself, modeling it on a riding whip that had hung above an old stone fireplace at the stables where I went riding. It was a style that's difficult to learn to use. But I hadn't known that, and so I'd gone about mastering it anyway. I knew how to place it precisely, to use it as a sting, a goad, a club, a knife's edge. I could caress with it, or set a back on fire. I could draw blood with it.

Now I trailed it over Celin's back and watched her tremble. She wasn't tied. I wanted to observe the speech of her body in response to the whip, unmuffled by restraints. I wanted to see if she'd accept it, or if she'd fight. Her body was clenched tight in anticipation of pain.

"Has anyone ever hit you before?"

"No . . . " Her voice was tight and choked.

I laid the whip on her back, slowly, gently, over, again. "How does it feel?"

She frowned. I could tell that she wanted to say, "It hurts," but it didn't, not yet. "It tickles," she reported, at length. Then she corrected herself. "Not tickles. It feels like being stroked."

"Being stroked?"

"Yes. Like with a hand." Her face relaxed. "It's nice," she said hesitantly.

"Mmm." I smiled.

I increased the force of my strokes, the leather now patting gently across her back. She sighed, closing her eyes, putting preconceptions behind her and feeling for the truth.

Her back took color slowly. The blush grew beneath the olive skin as the leather roughened its surface. Her face took on a similar glow. I could see her eyes moving rapidly behind their lids as the sensations were absorbed. She didn't notice when I crossed over the boundary between pleasure and pain. By then the rhythm was inescapable, the blows coming too fast for her to draw a proper breath between them. I worked in my favorite pattern, slowly down one side of the rib cage and back up the other, then down to stripe the ass.

At length she began to flinch and twist away from the lash. The smooth expression of her face broke into a grimace. I placed a hand on the back of her neck. "Still," I said softly. "Just for a moment more. Still."

She nodded and shivered, clenching her body tightly. I smiled, pleased, and laid the lash harder, counting down to myself as I watched her fight for her control: "—four, three, two, one!"

She cried out at the last blow, then lay shivering. I wrapped her in the thin blanket that I'd brought for that purpose. The training rooms were well-heated, so it wasn't really necessary. But it was comforting, I knew. I held her, automatically saying reassuring things: "You did well, little one, very well, very well. Rest now, you did well."

It was a full fifteen minutes before I realized I was no longer doing my job. I was, instead, doing my work.

One day, I decided to shave her. It was another good test of many things: docility, self-control, self-consciousness, reaction to embarrassing situations. Would she balk, would she hesitate? Would she grit her teeth and force herself through it? Would she welcome it?

I got a disposable razor out of my toolbag. The hair was long, a lifetime's growth. I used water and a small amount of gel. The razor tugged, raggedly severing the thick curling hairs close to the base. I heard her breath catch, then ease as she forced it back to an even rhythm. I stilled my hand on the razor and watched, fascinated, as the long muscles in her thighs jumped. All went smoothly until I got to the edges of the labia. That's always a tricky area. She whimpered but held still as I parted the lips to shave their inner edges. Another coat of gel, a final pass to take the hair down as close as it would go, and she was done.

I stepped back and surveyed my work. "Nice. Very nice. I like it."

She raised her head cautiously. "Master? May I see?"

I nodded permission, and she sat up, bending her head forward and peering at her groin. Her eyes widened at the sight. She reached a tentative finger and touched the naked pink pubic mound. "Wow!" she breathed.

I smiled. "Like it?"

She nodded, still staring at her pubis.

"What does it look like?" I pressed.

"I look like a little girl," she said slowly, blushing.

I laughed. "Yes. You do. Bigger, but like a little girl." I

reached down and gently flicked the labia with a fingertip. "So pretty, like flower petals."

She smiled, a gradual shy smile. "It is, isn't it, Master? Pretty."

"Mm-hmm." I eased onto the couch next to her, stroking a finger up and down the crevice between the lips. My mouth was next to her ear, my breath ruffling the short hairs on her neck as I spoke. "Some masters like this. Some will want you shaved because it's cleaner. Some like it because it's easier to see and feel you. And some like it because it makes you look like a little girl." She was moist now, and I increased the pressure slightly, teasing at the opening. "It helps that you're small," I said, easing a finger inside her, hearing her sharply indrawn breath with satisfaction. "Small, and tight, and sensitive. Squeeze me."

She bit her lip and began to contract her pelvic muscles rhythmically, her forehead wrinkled in concentration. "Relax," I ordered. "It's not hard. Relax and breathe. You have the muscles, now use them."

She took a deep breath, and I felt the tension go out of her. Then she relaxed, letting her muscles loose. Then another deep breath, like a tidal surge, and I was amazed at the sudden strength of the gripping muscles. And she released it, and I felt her cunt gape wider than I'd ever felt it. I almost missed my opportunity, but seized it just in time and slipped in a second finger. She gripped it on the next breath, smiling as she did so, then let it go. I fell into an easy rhythm, deep as her breathing, surging and retreating, opening her wider, wider, ever wider. "Open to me," I chanted softly, "Open to me, my slave, my little one. That's it, keep going, you're doing so well. Give to me, open to me." Gently, slowly, with the tides and patience of the ocean, I moved into her.

I stopped at three fingers. She was full, taut and high with the pleasure of it, but not stretched. Stretching her would be a pleasure, indeed: placing my fingers inside her, opening my hand and feeling the ring of muscle tighten around my wrist like a band of living steel. Watching her hurt and sweat, impaled on my hand. But now she was a little girl, to be treated gently. The one who bought her could tear her at will. She wasn't mine to be taken in that way.

Another whipping. This time I planned to push her, to see if she struggled against me, against the whip, or with herself.

I was working with a variety of implements, pausing in between to show them to her, explain their uses, and let her feel their differences. I was generous, letting her state preferences and encouraging her to develop a liking for certain tools. She liked clamps, so I placed a line of them along her inner thighs, ending on her labia, and then flicked them off one by one with a small cat. She let out little yelps at each one. I smiled and caressed the butterfly-shaped welts before selecting a larger whip and going to work on her back.

She accepted the whip easily this time, actually smiling as it started to land. I pushed. She flowed with me. I pushed harder, listening to her sighs and small noises as she slipped along the line between sensations, where she was learning to enjoy herself so much. Her back was glowing, red, radiating heat.

And I saw the whip slash out, crosshatching her ribs with long red weals, one, two, three, four, five, six. I saw them start to drip. She screamed and started to struggle, as I smiled and prepared to repeat the lashes on the other side—

"Master?" She raised her head. "Why did you stop?"

The faint bluish light through the nearly drawn blinds lay across her back. The skin over her ribs formed a smooth, unbroken pattern of light and dark.

I dropped the whip. I tried to speak and failed. I stared at her.

"Master?" She tugged against the bonds, starting to sound upset. "Master, are you all right?"

"I'm fine." Without untying her, I tossed a blanket over her. "You lie quiet, now." She subsided, relaxing under the blanket, still glowing and high from the beating.

Back when I was doing this for free, I would occasionally be approached by a novice who wanted to know how to be a good dominant. I'd insist that they should examine their own heart's desire, and craft their own style based on that. No one was pleased with that answer, so after a while I got exasperated and refused to respond. But I could never understand why my answer wasn't good enough. It seemed to me to be a denial of self-knowledge. Why would anyone want that?

Now I had a reason all of my own. I knew what I wanted, I just couldn't have it. My self-knowledge was no longer any help to me.

She was sleeping. Her soft breathing filled the room. I undressed quietly and rummaged in my toolbag. The leather harness slipped on easily. I chose a long, relatively slender dildo with a slightly enlarged head. I crouched beside the table, cupping the dildo in my hands to warm it up.

She stirred as I slipped under the blanket. "Master, what—"

I climbed on top of her, caressing her back. "Shhh. Lie still. I want to fuck you."

She sighed and relaxed. Even though the bonds held her tight, I could sense a new yielding, a liquid quality to her body. Her hips swiveled easily as I parted her thighs, pressing in between them. She was wet. I felt the now-familiar paths under my fingers, gathered the growing wetness and spread it on the head of the dildo. I guided it to the entrance, nudged it gently past the point of resistance, and then thrust it deep. She gasped as I probed against the resilient core of her cervix. Her ass was still warm from the beating. I lowered my head and set my teeth into the flesh of her shoulder. She hissed in pain and I released her, mindful that I mustn't break skin. She made a small noise of frustration and tried to push back as I slowly withdrew, teasing her opening with the dildo's head. I laughed. "Greedy, aren't you? Do you like it?"

I could barely see the gleam of her teeth in the semi-darkness as she smiled. Her voice was thick with desire. "Yes, Master. I like it."

"Good." I grinned and slammed into her. My clit jumped as the dildo collided with her cervix again, again, battering her. I wanted to hurt her, I meant to hurt her, I wanted her to remember me every time she touched herself. I wanted her to carry my bruises for days. She was gasping and crying out, but not fighting me, and I fucked her exactly as I pleased.

My orgasm came surprisingly fast. I groaned and let it take me, let it shake me violently as it ground itself out against her body. As always, the aftermath was almost better than the orgasm itself. I wrapped myself around her, clinging to her skin, searching for the breaks that I knew were not there, seeking to warm my cold belly in her blood. It had been so long, so very long.

A tear dripped onto the reddened skin. I held her and cried silently, praying that she wouldn't notice. If she did, she said nothing.

She was a good slave.

Mal stopped me in the hall the next morning. "Shum, about that life contract, Celin. She's still on your schedule."

It wasn't a question. "Yes, she is."

Mal looked impatient. "Is there a problem? You've had her six weeks now."

"There's no problem. She's coming along nicely. She just needs more polish, that's all." Mal made a discontented sound, and I hastened to add, "Six weeks isn't that long to train a slave, Mal. Not for a life contract."

"I suppose." She didn't sound happy. "Just keep it moving along, will you, Shum? The bank wants their money. They want to schedule an auction soon."

I stopped by a fruit market on the way to work. The fruit was beautiful, piled in fragrant pyramids of emerald and ruby and tangerine, the sort of produce that no one could afford anymore on a regular basis. I purchased a large, absurdly perfect apple and watched as it was painstakingly wrapped in cushioning tissue. I told myself that I wasn't spoiling her. Her master would, no doubt, give her treats on occasion, and learning to show proper appreciation was part of her training. I had no idea whether she liked apples or not. That reassured me as to my motivations. It was part of her training, and nothing more: learning to be grateful for a gift or favor, no matter if it was what she really wanted.

She was kneeling when I entered the training room. She bowed her head to the floor. I watched her critically, noting the ways in which her posture had improved, approving of the soft yet clear tone of her voice as she greeted me.

"I brought something for you, slave." She looked up, startled, then dropped her gaze again, taking refuge in silence and the trained posture.

I removed the tissue-wrapped apple from my bag and held it out to her. "Go on. Take it."

She hesitated again, but reached out and took the package from my hands. Unwrapping it tentatively, she gave a gasp of delight when the apple was revealed. Her eyes glowed. "Thank you, Master."

I wanted to kiss her. I wanted to hug her, to reach out and ruffle her hair as she joyously devoured the apple and licked the juice off her chin. My mind flashed back to the fruit market and I imagined the glowing mound of oranges, and I wondered if she'd like one of those, too.

Then I caught myself. I cleared my throat and said sternly, "Your appreciation is proper, slave, but I am not your master. Remember that. I am only your trainer, and this is part of your training, to learn proper thankfulness and appreciation."

The joy went out of her eyes. She ducked her head and knelt in silence as I continued with my speech, hating every word. When I called her attention to the forgotten apple, she ate it mechanically; when I was done speaking, she thanked me politely for the instruction, in a small quiet voice. I was so angry with myself. I'd wanted to give her a treat. She'd responded perfectly—with appreciation for a master's thoughtfulness. And I'd spoiled it.

She obeyed me perfectly throughout the rest of the session. I forgot what we worked on—positioning, I think it was, and I also gave her a monotonous, dispassionate flogging. Elementary material, all of it. Things that both of us could do in our sleep. When I was done and about to leave, she thanked me again for the instruction. All along, her eyes were downcast, her face sad.

Mal intercepted me in the hallway outside the training room. "Shum, how are you? I've been meaning to talk to you—"

I decided to pretend I was sick, to try to avoid the encounter. "I'm not well, Mal, I really think I need to go home and lie down."

"Oh." She hesitated, then blurted out, "Shum, that life contract—it's been two months now, we really need to set a sale date, the bank has been calling—"

I gritted my teeth. "You might as well go ahead and schedule it. She's as ready as she'll ever be."

Mal frowned. "I don't understand. Do you mean she's not—"

"No, no, Mal, she's fine. She'll be a credit to the House, really. Now please, excuse me, I must go."

She stepped aside in haste. Feigning a stomach ailment can dislodge the most persistent questioners. "Of course, Shum, and thank you. Stay home and rest until you feel better."

I stumbled outside the House and started down the

street. The wind was cold, the winter day clear and bright. In the shadow of the Obelisk a sudden cramp bent me over, and I thought of self-fulfilling prophecies as I struggled against nausea.

"She's not yours," I said aloud over the ringing in my ears. "She isn't yours." Her price was far beyond my means. If I worked ten years at my current wage, saving every penny, I couldn't hope to buy her.

The cramp intensified suddenly and I fell to the pavement, stunned at the sheer knife-edged pain of it. Then, just as quickly, it eased, and I drew a deep breath and sobbed with relief. And then I was sobbing for real, crying, heartbroken, scrabbling with my hands in the dead leaves piled against the base of the Obelisk, looking for something that was lost.

A hand on my shoulder. "Miss? Miss, are you all right?"

Of course I'm not all right, you fool, I wanted to say. Instead I nodded, sitting back on my heels to dust myself off, waving away the concerned-looking young man who was trying to help me.

"I'm fine," I said, standing unsteadily.

"I'm just fine," walking down the street, not looking where I was going. "Just fine."

We did the filming the next day. Celin hadn't been rehearsed at all, and Mal was worried. Celin wasn't, and neither was I. All she had to do was obey. I took her through her paces quickly and efficiently. I knew how to show a slave to good advantage. Celin stayed focused on my commands, refusing to be distracted by the camera. I knew that that quality would come out well on the tape, and it did. Mal congratulated me with a broad smile and then gave orders for extra copies to be made.

Celin was sold within the week. Mal and the bank were both pleased, Mal going as far as to invite me into her office for a glass of champagne. "As always, your judgment was excellent, Shum," she said, raising her glass to me. "You've really done a splendid job with her."

"Yes." I had. She was my best work ever.

"I'm giving you a raise," she continued. "I'm going to see if I can't get you some more work like that."

I placed my glass down on an end table, carefully, so it wouldn't break. "I don't think so, Mal. I'm burned out. I need a rest."

Mal frowned. "Well, of course. Take a few weeks. We can always talk about this another time."

"Yes. Another time."

I went to see Celin in her cubicle. She was sitting on the bed, resting, waiting. As I came in she looked up, startled, then quickly knelt. Her voice was pleased. "It's good to see you, Master."

I didn't know what to say. It's good to see you, too? Good-bye? Don't forget to write? Why didn't you take the fucking job at the Burger Hut so I could at least have you in the evenings? I cleared my throat. "I came to say good-bye, Celin."

"I know." She smiled. "Thank you for everything, Master."

My throat hurt. I prayed that I'd be able to speak without croaking. "Don't call me that any more, Celin. I'm not your master."

"I know, Master."

It was a deliberate disobedience, one that I'd have slapped her for a day before. Now I merely nodded. "You'll do well, Celin. You'll do well."

"I know, Master." There was pride in her voice. "You trained me."

I smiled, and oh, it hurt. "I have to go now. Be well, Celin."

"Be well, Master."

I left the House for good that day. I haven't been back. I run into some of the trainers at the clubs from time to time. They are cordial, if not friendly, and Fan and I are still occasional lovers. Silver Roland tried to recruit me for her House for a while. She finally gave up when I took a full-time job as a landscaper. Now all I train are shrubs and small flowering trees. One day, I think, I'd like to go back to the work that is in my blood, if I can find a way to do it as I did it before, more humbly and more freely.

But first, I need to let the world pass me by.

WIDE OPEN

Le Shaun

IT'S FUNNY. MALE groupies are intimidated by me. They don't step to me like the female groupies step to the male rappers. You have the bold ones who talk to their homies and they're like "I'ma push on up her, I'm gonna hit that," but then when they come up to me they got to come on correct or I'm gonna dis 'em. I find it really hard to find someone I can chill with. I kind of want to go back with ex-boyfriends cause they knew me before and they understood me. Now I have a reputation for being the Black Widow, so guys are intimidated by me, they're scared. I'm very dominant, and I just take control. They feel themselves getting smaller and smaller by the minute. But they don't have to. They let me treat them that way. And so I do.

This weekend I told this guy who I knew for years, I said to him, I really like you. I want to like you, I want to be with you. When he started acting funny, I told him, I said, I really could like you, but I'm not gonna put up with your bull, if you tell me you're gonna do something, then do it. I told him I let my guard down for him, and he thought it was humorous. I told him I coulda treated him like a bitch, like any other nigger that come into my life, and he's taking it for granted. He doesn't know how serious I am. I like him, but I'm not gonna let him walk all over me. If you say you're gonna call me at a certain time, I expect you to call me within thirty minutes, otherwise I'm gonna get up and leave, just so I won't be there when you call an hour or two later. I'm trying to figure out if he really likes me or if he wants to see if he can be the one man to break me. It's the same thing for me. I told him what I wanted, and then when he wasn't taking me seriously, I went to see him and flipped it. I was trying to control him and his whole domain by cursing him out, I got to get my points back. I go and I'm cursing him out, then I'm out of here, and then I'm stuck saying he better come after me. He did. He was like, oh, it's like that, huh?

One guy and I, we wuz just doing foreplay, and then my phone rang. I got on the phone and said hello and before I finished the conversation he had already put it in and came, that fast. I just said get off of me. I was mad. He wasted my time. All this foreplay and every-thing, it's not just for one person. He wasn't worried about pleasing me, just himself. I know I'm the woman and shit, but damn, you couldn't give me two or three minutes? I gave him another chance to prove himself, and he fucked it up even worse. He felt so stupid. Every time he get up in it, he's just gonna do the same. He can't handle it. He doin' something wrong. If we doin' it, and he gives me about fifteen minutes for the first nut and then he comes, that's alright, and then we go on to the second one. I handle my part, and by the second one, he better handle his. I'm not gonna come in the first fifteen minutes. Usually they come and then it takes a while for me. He gets the first one off, and then he gotta concentrate that I'm satisfied. They're some guys I just want to fuck up, fuck their head up, everything, I don't want to come, I don't concentrate, so they know they can't fuck with me, I'm finished, I'll see you later, leave the nigger there going damn, I can't make her come.

Then you got your brothers who can fuck you all up. There was one who fucked me all up, made me come twice. What made it worse he didn't even come the first time. I felt he had stripped me of my crown, left me wide open. I was like, I want to marry him. I'm gonna get his ass. I know he did it on purpose. You know how guys pull out when they don't want to come, so they stop it, and when you stop it so many times it won't come out. He kept doing that. The fact that he had that much control fucked me up. Here I am, I'm supposed to be the Black Widow, I'm supposed to be so dope, and this motherfucker comes along and throws a monkey wrench into my whole shit. Now I'm like, I gotta get him. I gotta sit down, think of my strategy, watch a couple of pornos, then git it. I'm a gonna get him. Until this point I never met anyone who was a match for me. I met guys who satisfied me, but he took me to a whole new level.

I do the "ritual" to everybody, I just love ass. I flip them over, feel their ass, then pretend like I'm the man, sometimes I use my fingers or lick them down there. I let them lick my shit and the whole ritual, and then I'll hump on them, do the "wide open." Some brothers tell me from jump, I'll break your fucking fingers if you think of sticking them up my ass. I have nice fingers, with three-inch nails. Even though they're three inches long, the nails don't hurt, 'cause they're thinner than my fingers and they're not sharp. Other niggers, they enjoy it, they let me go all the way, wide open. Some say stop, but I calm them down, they be so tense they be locking up. Usually I won't see them afterward, I can't even look at them, I lose all respect. If a guy lets me do it, if he really enjoys it, then I feel like he could be gay. Now that my song "Wide Open" is out, guys think twice about saying they slept with me.

PRE - DAHMER

Trac Vu

THE FIRST TIME I ever chewed gum, it was in Sai Gon after the communists took over. Food was scarce. We were constantly hungry. My brother's friend's aunt abroad sent his family a shipment that contained a pack of Spearmint. Strawberry flavor, or something sweet like that. When my brother got back with the loot, it was late at night, a couple of hours after dinner, which we had stretched to no end: five people had shared an omelette made with two eggs and nineteen tomatoes. When I started chewing on the Spearmint, sugar released on my tongue. I wanted to swallow the gum right then and there, eat it like I would a piece of meat. But I knew that I couldn't, that gum was for chewing, that eventually I'd have to spit it back out, in one piece. That's what it was like sucking a guy for the first time.

from THE SPIRIT THAT DENIES

Jay Michaelson

As we left 495 for I-270 toward Frederick, I noticed that Samantha was unusually quiet. Shifting into fourth, I skipped lanes.

"How are you feeling?" I asked. She smiled nervously.

"Okay. Kind of jittery." She brushed an errant lock of reddish-brown hair from her eyes. "Like butterflies." I smiled.

"This is nothing."

"I know."

"The Feast is more," I groped for the words, glancing quickly in the rearview mirror as I cut sharply into the left lane, accelerated, "—intense. *Much* more intense. This is just a preview." She nodded, settled deeper into her seat.

I decided the best way to start was with an animal.

THE SPIRIT THAT DENIES

While a human would have been better, the possibility
of disease was an active concern; Sam lacked my immu-
nity to the ills of man and beast. Of course, even with
animals there was risk, but since the nastiest parasites
were either organ- or host-specific, she could avoid the
worst by sticking to the flesh and blood. Hydatid tape-
worms in the lungs, flukes in the liver and intestine, et
cetera.

We sped up 270 until we came to a place I deemed
suitable, several miles up the Potomac, near Clarksburg.
I knew this was a good area for herbivores.

I parked the car and stepped out, sniffing the air. I
could smell life. Good.

I pulled the car back onto the grass and covered it
with some fallen branches, a nearby pine tree donating
some fresh ones. I removed the license plates and threw
them in the backseat. I locked up and backed off, looking at it from a distance.

"Nobody'll notice that." I turned to Sam.

"Are you warm enough?" She nodded, her coat pulled
tight about her shoulders, her hands in her pockets.

"Uh-huh," she said brightly, smiling despite her ner-
vousness. "It's not that cold out."

"Not to me," I snorted. "but I didn't know *you* liked it
in the low fifties."

"It's not that cold out," she said with more conviction.

We headed deeper into the forest and I kept sniffing.
After walking about twenty minutes we came to a clearing that was remote enough for our purpose. I undressed, folding my clothes in a neat pile.

"Do you have any serious dental work? Bridges?
Caps?" She looked surprised by the mundanity of the
question.

"Uh—No, not at all. Just some fillings." She opened her mouth for my inspection. I dismissed it with a wave.

"You'll want to take off your coat for this," I said, and she looked forlorn. "But not until I get back. There's no point to freezing you now. Do you meditate?"

"Of course," she said in a voice that said I was silly for asking.

"Then start doing so now. I'm not entirely sure how to go about this. You're going to the Feast in less than a month, and this is to help prepare you. Here's what I want you to do." I approached her, my face and hers almost meeting. "Think about me. Concentrate on what it means to be a wolf." I tapped my temple. "Try to get inside my head." She stared at me intently, her eyes following me carefully. I could already taste blood, and running my hand over the back of my forearm yielded a greasy feel; the pores were generating oil, starting to Change. "I'm going to Change now. Watch."

I dropped to my knees, my body shifting and stretching. I groaned sharply, my oily flesh sprouting hair, my body itching terribly over every inch of skin. I opened my mouth in agony, drooling inadvertently, my saliva lit with streaks of blood as my teeth reformed, shifted within my skull, pushed out, grew longer. Ahhhhhhh! The Pain! The Torture! My very bones stretching, my frightened flesh screaming with delight. As my skull made ominous pops and cracks, the amplified sounds like explosions in my head, I reflected upon what a masochist I must be to enjoy this, to actually welcome the Change. But I did, as do we all. Despite or perhaps because of the pain it was a tremendous relief to shift back into full form, my true form! Ah, God! Much like the pain of teething, I suppose. A stinging ache, a scrape of flesh and blood, but what relief after! Like the sweetest pain, an aching delight . . .

Like slipping into a warm bath at the end of a hard day. Only my bath is . . . full of needles . . .

I writhed on the ground, my agonized flesh twitching spastically across my doubled frame. My arms and legs changed proportion, the femurs warping within their muscular insertions and origins, grating noisily. I felt like a living marionette, my strings pulled by the harshest hand biology had to offer.

After several minutes of twitching and twisting beneath the assaults of my renegade physiology, I was complete. The death of the man, the Re-Birth of the Wolf. I got unsteadily to my feet, fresh strength coursing through my veins along with a gnawing ache in my stomach, the call of hunger. I stood on all fours, complete, a whole being once again, no longer trapped in that ridiculously limited human frame, nor within my half-man-half-wolf shape. After stretching happily, the fresh cartilage within my spine adamantly refusing to pop, I fell back on my haunches and tossed my head skyward, uttering a joyous howl, my long, white teeth feeling fresh and new, the otherwise pristine enamel streaked with blood. I turned to regard Samantha. I padded closer to her, my lips curved back in the only smile I could make, a carnivorous grin.

"What-do-you-think?" I growled, the words harsh and barely English. It was difficult to maintain human vocal chords within a canine body, and the strain made my throat raw. I could see the sun racing to meet the horizon over Sam's shoulder. A pity. I loved to hunt in the full daylight.

"You are beautiful," she said, her voice soft and awed. She put her hand out to touch my shoulder, her fingers brushing my fur. She looked as though she were about to start crying the way she did the first time I Changed for her. "This is—" she broke off, swallowed hard, started again. "This is too good to be real." I panted at her, my breath still invisible in the cool air.

"But-it-is," I growled. "I-go-now." I said, my throat tiring. Withholding any select organ from change was very difficult to maintain, like balancing precariously on a fence; the first time your attention wanes you find yourself on the ground, a few bruises wiser. I headed into the forest.

"Jack?" she called. I glanced back. "Good luck."

The first deer I caught was a stag; I devoured him, tearing his throat out and then making short work of the rest. I had the feeling of being under a deadline, because I wanted to finish my meal and catch a deer for Samantha. Maybe that was what was spoiling my normally buoyant mood.

Whatever it was, it didn't last long. After feeding on the stag, I felt the rush of strength and bliss along with the temporary abatement of appetite; satiated, I continued to sniff the wind and follow tracks.

I found another deer soon after. I would have liked to herd her back to the grove, but to do that I needed at least one partner, preferably two. The only way of getting her back alive was to shift to biped, knock her unconscious and carry her back to Sam slung over my shoulders. Despite the waste of time I couldn't see any other way.

I shifted, moving toward her odor when I was done.

After sizing up the terrain I dashed toward the doe and she bounded away with almost equal speed, her leaps delicate and precise. I caught her exactly twenty-five feet from where I spotted her, tackling her and clopping her on the head just hard enough to knock her out without killing her.

Shouldering the limp form, I began my jog back to the grove. As I ran I could feel the pulse-beat of her heart warming me between my shoulder blades.

I reentered the clearing gripping the now-conscious and struggling doe by the legs. I strode forward, knowing by smell that no one was there except Samantha. Good thing, too. Sam would have had a hell of a time explaining what she was doing in a grove meditating next to a pile of clothing. Heh.

Despite my silence she looked up, her eyes widening as I approached. I knelt down and placed the doe before her on the ground.

"Eat," I said, shifting my vocal chords enough to talk. "You-must-kill-her. With-your-teeth." Sam didn't look at me as she took off her coat. She threw it aside and knelt before the doe, who by this time had redoubled her efforts at freedom. To no avail; my hands remained clamped on her legs, two in each hand. Samantha crouched down next to me, looking to me for guidance. I turned to face her.

"You-must . . . relish-the-taste-of-blood-and-meat . . . to-join-Family-you-must-learn. Feed!" I choked out, my voice hoarse. She was listening to me, her attentions torn between the squirming doe and myself. "None of-the-sensations-that-accompany-this-life," I thumped my chest. "will be-buffered. If-you-desire-it-then-proceed." I couldn't bear to tell her, couldn't bear to think that if she failed this test, tradition dictated that I should kill her.

She took her brown eyes from my blue ones, glanced at the doe. Then, without a word, she bent her head to the doe's struggling neck. While I pressed my elbow against the flailing head to hold it down, Samantha placed her open mouth on the doe's flesh, the thick fur insufficient armor against Sam's teeth. As I watched, my heart rejoicing, the doe gave a shrill cry and blood welled up around Sam's mouth, flowing down the side of the deer's neck. Even though Sam wasn't biting in the correct place to cause death, I hadn't corrected her because it would be best if this were messy, if it lacked precision. I wanted her to see the worst side; to feel the grueling labor, not the pleasant sensation of a well-dispatched kill. It was seldom a single act that could be done quickly, anyway; in real life, it was work. A battle between the intensity of your hunger and the will-to-live of the other creature. After she had taken a bite of the flesh and managed to work it loose with her teeth she swallowed it, looking at me with pride.

"Right-here," I growled, indicating it with a claw, "is-where-life flows. Here-you-must-bite." I guided her mouth by hand and she bit, her eagerness apparent. The deer let out a terrified shriek and Sam chewed with increasing viciousness, digging her teeth in, moving her head back and forth in the correct rending fashion.

As the blood welled forth in vigorous spurts, Sam tore harder, biting savagely at the resistant tissue. She lifted her face to me, her chin and teeth streaked with blood, her cheeks smeared with the deer's moistness, and I realized she was reaching the tough muscle that enshrouded the deer's major cables. Soon after that she would be hitting the cartilaginous parts of the throat and trachea, and would have more difficulties owing to the generalized nature of her teeth.

While I watched she continued taking small bites from the doe's neck, the blood welling out in crimson brilliance and pouring onto the ground. The doe squealed and blood gushed, and I knew that unless I helped her we were going to lose that most delicate pearl of great price, the special moment when the doe crossed between life and death. I pulled her head up and tugged the doe's slackening form closer to me so that we could both partake of her throat. Blood was pumping in weakening surges from the poorly inflicted wounds, the deer's thrombin making itself useful.

"Bite-with-me," I said, pulling her head next to mine on the doe's neck. I could feel her gory cheek pressed against my lips as I sank my teeth into the tender flesh, tasting the deer's death as I pierced her jugular and left carotid. I tasted hot surges of salt iron as I drew my razor teeth through her dying flesh. I could feel Samantha's mouth next to mine, drinking the blood as I raked my teeth away, rending the doe still further, leaving her neck a pulped mess that was more accessible to Sam's small, primate mouth. It was difficult to do, because I could feel the joy of the doe's life gushing out, forcing its way through my nerves, but I wanted Samantha to have it; it was for her. This was her first time.

I withdrew, my mouth ripe with the taste of life, and watched Sam dig her mouth deeper into the deer. The doe's thrashing was weakening enough that I no longer had to hold her legs as Sam tore the remnants of life from her. I watched as she fed, her movements less shaky, her hunger abating. I knew without a doubt that she was of the blood.

Feeling my own hunger rising again, I began tearing at the rib cage with my hands, breaking the bones and stripping the inner meats when Samantha tried to join me.

"No. You-eat-only-the-neck." Without a word she moved back to the neck and continued feeding there.

Together we made short work of the doe, Sam eating her flesh while I devoured everything else. After another few minutes almost nothing remained but the bones.

When we were done I sat back gnawing a femur, satiated. This was the second time I had fed in under an hour. I felt the onset of a drowsy euphoria, my adrenaline pump having dissipated. With a flex of my humanoid hands I broke the bone in half and chewed the marrow thus exposed. I felt good.

Samantha crawled to me, her eyes lit with the euphoria that comes from the direct assimilation of another's life; the joy in partaking of the Sacrament of Flesh, that we of the Family feel after feeding. I reached forward to put a hand on her shoulder. She moved into my arms, the lower half of her face covered with blood, her teeth reddened pearls mounted in ruby gums.

"You-are-of-the-blood," I said, blood singing in my veins. "You will-do-well-at-the-Feast." She looked into my eyes with a feverish intensity, her gaze sighting down my snout and ending in my brain. Then, much to my surprise, she put her mouth to mine and kissed me.

I was both surprised and dizzy; I wanted to back away, to ask why, to request an explanation. Instead I sat there and held her, staring at her with open shock.

She reached up and gripped my head with both hands, her fingers entwining in my fur, pulling my mouth closer. She kissed me again, with more passion this time, biting my lower lip, her tongue touching mine. Even in my distraction I couldn't fail to notice that the wildly disparate design of our mouths presented difficulties. She continued despite the obvious difference of the analogous structures, her determined amorousness brooking no dissension, even from Mother Nature.

She nibbled at my lower lip, then lifted her head and kissed me on the nose, the face, the snout. With a soft groan I met her tongue with mine, gripping her tighter about the waist and licking at her mouth, my own passion growing. She squirmed in my lap as my arousal became more evident. I could smell her sharp pungency and knew that the odor of her sex would enslave me if I smelled it much longer. I had a brief vision of a pack of baying wolves, the screams of the others around me, firelight, blood. . . . She was still kissing me, her hands exploring my body, caressing my shoulders and sides, my arms and neck. I was fearful of what was happening but no longer possessed the strength to push her away. She had removed her shirt at some point, and I groaned as I felt her half-naked body pressing tightly against my furred chest, her breasts soft and arousing. I tried to stand up, knowing I could take no more.

"Oh-God-no," I groaned. "No . . ." She stopped, taking her mouth from mine and regarding me.

"What's the matter, Jack?" she said, her voice heady with revealed desires. I looked at her with panic bordering on fear, my heart pounding. She reached up and stroked my head, her touch warm and soothing.

"I—we—can't," was all I could say. She kept stroking my forehead, her touch gentle. She looked at me, waited for me to go on. "You-don't-know," I finished in a weak and tremulous voice. She perked up.

"Don't know what, Jack? What don't I know?" She said with surprising vigor. I looked at her with amazement.

"Our-bodies," I managed to choke out. Much to my horror, she gave me a feral smile, stuck her tongue out, and touched the tip of my nose. I groaned, moved to even further distraction by her casual manner.

"Is *that* what's bothering you?" She said in gentle amazement. "The difference in our bodies? Don't worry!" She reassured me. I shook my head.

"You-don't-understand," I reaffirmed. "I-can't—" I paused, my tongue thick in my mouth. I swallowed hard. "I-can't-do-it-any-other way. Than-in-the-body-of-a-wolf. I-can't-turn-human-now. I-can't-even hold-this-form-much-longer." I said, feeling ashamed, my gruff voice pathetic in my own ears. She smiled.

"What's so wrong with doing it like this?" She asked, her voice gentle but distracting. I groaned as she ground her pelvis against me, her sex rubbing the furry sheath that housed my penis, her motion exciting me beyond endurance. I could feel her moisture working into my fur.

"Canine-physiology," was all I could say, my voice hoarse, my throat raw.

"Ohhh," she said in a soft voice. "*I* know what's bothering you. My silly Jack," she continued stroking my forehead. "You're embarrassed, aren't you?" I couldn't answer. She kissed me again on the nose.

"You think I don't know about Canine Physiology?"

she said, putting emphasis on the last two words. "Don't know what? You mean I don't know how it is that you fuck? You mean I don't know that after you penetrate me the base of your penis . . ." She grabbed my sheath, her fingers enfolding it. I groaned, and my erection sprang forth into her grasp. ". . . will swell once it's inside me until it's sooo big you won't be able to remove it until you're done? Done—" her voice became huskier, "—Done fucking me? You think I don't know that after it's . . ." She paused, licking her lips. ". . . fully swollen, you'll turn about and fuck me from behind, facing away from me, our rear ends stuck together like two dogs in—" I howled to silence her. She stopped. I gave a disconsolate groan, my emotions impossible to assess, but including the acute desire to vanish into the ground. My feelings alternating between elation and horror, I wondered if turning to vapor and dissipating in the evening air was too much to ask.

"I-love-you," I growled, only realizing it was my voice as I said it. I felt very strange. With a tender expression she put her hand on my neck and kissed me on the mouth.

"I love you, too," she said, and put her mouth to my ear.

"It's not that I know and it doesn't bother me; it's that I know . . ." She nipped the lower part of my ear. ". . . and I want to. I really *want* to."

I don't remember the rest as clearly as I'd like to. I gave in with a groan and attacked her, licking her face and neck. Not the best way to show my passion, I suppose, but that's what I could do. She resumed her inflammatory motions against me, her legs straddling my waist, her hands working their way around my body.

"Jack?" she asked, her voice tentative. I grunted in response.

"You're hurting me," she said, grabbing my wrists.

"Sorry," I grunted, loosening my grip. I hadn't meant to squeeze her so tightly. She smiled to show me it was all right, and continued moving atop me.

I pushed her down to the ground and crawled atop her. I was Changing as I did so, unable to muster the concentration necessary to hold myself between forms. She noticed, and said: "It's okay, Jack. It really is." And I finished Changing, her hands playing over my shifting body.

She lay on the ground, watching me as I regained my true shape. I padded over her, my head near hers, and she kissed me again. I whined and retreated until my head was near her crotch. She had removed her jeans while I Changed, and I put my paw to her panties and pulled them down. She spread her legs farther apart and gasped, our mutual anticipation leaving our perceptions flushed, our combined desires almost palpable.

Without further ado I lowered my head to her crotch and gave it the same treatment I had given her face and neck, snuffling at her sex. Her flesh tasted sweet, the tang of her vagina different from but reminiscent of her whole body, her life. She shuddered and moaned as I licked and nipped at her flesh. I looked up at her, stopping to see her reaction.

"Oh God," she panted. "Go on!"

I lowered my head back to her body, planting my forepaws on either side of her. I lapped at her, my big, flat tongue too clumsy to do anything really spectacular to her clitoris. Running my tongue up her thigh, one of my teeth accidentally raked across her smooth skin, tracing a thin welt of blood. She cried out, both hands on my head.

"Jack!" she said, her voice on the edge of delirium. "Don't stop! Oh God!" I put my mouth back to her vagina, her body shivering with taut spasms beneath my lustful ministrations.

I wasn't able to keep this up for very long before I was in a frenzy. Not that I was any too calm to start with, but touching her, smelling her, and tasting her was all too much. I stood above her, panting and pawing at her to turn over so I could mount her when she gave me a wicked smile and moved forward beneath me.

My hips were already in motion, thrusting of their own accord at the air. I yapped despite myself as her hand encountered my penis, wrapping around the shaft of my erection, the retracted sheath bunched up behind the growing bulge at the base, exposing the tender, pink flesh to view.

"Ohhh," she said from beneath me. "It's so—different." If I was in human form I would have flushed bright crimson, but all I could manage was to pant and wish that I could fall into the ground and have it close seamlessly after my passage.

I whined as her hands stroked up and down, one hand cradling my testicles while the other stroked my penis and the surrounding skin. Noticing my discomfort, Sam surfaced on one side of me, her face flushed and grinning.

"Jack," she said sweetly, "you aren't still embarrassed, are you?" I just looked away, caught between my fierce biological desire, my feelings for her, and the last tattered shreds of human pride I had left. Yes, I was embarrassed.

I felt her hand creeping around my neck, turning me gently back to face her. She looked up at me and said in a voice I could not doubt:

"I love you." She leaned up and kissed me on the mouth. "And," she considered, looking into my eyes, "you love me, whether you can say so right now or not. Am I right?" I struggled within myself, trying to fight off my disordering lust long enough to reform my throat just to say—

"I-do. Love-you. Oh-God-I-do. Samantha," I said, the words emphasized by the undue harshness with which I said them. And I did. Love her, I mean. She smiled.

"Then it's all right." With another wicked grin, she slid back under me. "And don't be embarrassed. You're not only beautiful, but you have more to brag about than any man I've ever seen."

If I could have talked, I would have told her that flattery could get her anywhere, at least with me. Instead I backed up onto my haunches and threw my head skyward and howled. *Really* howled. The kind of howl that would leave humans shaking in their sleep, warn every animal in a twenty-mile radius that they had better get away from her *now* and not come back; and (I hoped) display my sentiment at having Samantha stroke my decidedly male ego. She smiled, kissed me again, then went back to fondling me.

She continued studying my anatomy, making appreciative noises at appropriate intervals, until I was ready to go insane. My heart was about to tear itself free from my chest while my hips were pumping and jerking despite my best efforts to curb their motions. Samantha was kind enough not to laugh. I finally backed away from her pleasant touch, and growled commandingly.

She either understood my growl or saw the feral gleam in my eye, because she immediately got to her hands and knees, presenting me with her ass.

I managed to wait until she had braced herself, her ass lowered a little, her legs firmly planted, before leaping upon her, my erection prodding at her vagina, frantic at my attempts to enter. She gasped.

"Need some help back there?" she said, her voice husky with need. In the midst of my ineffective thrusting I felt her fingers on the tip of my cock, her hand reaching between her legs, guiding the tip. I felt my cock in contact with her wetness, tried to restrain myself from too brutal a thrust, and failed. She gasped and shivered beneath me. I clutched her waist with my forelegs while my pelvis went crazy. I whined and pushed myself into her, my pleasure increasing a thousandfold.

The first difficulty was when I realized that the base of my penis was already partially swollen, and I would have to force the bulge into her. She knew it, too, and I felt her body tense beneath me as the engorged base bumped against her vaginal lips. I kept my thrusts as gentle as I could, barely in control of the process, and I knew that I was just going to have to let it happen.

Through the haze that was threatening to eclipse my consciousness, I heard her cry out, and realized I had entered her all the way. I hoped I hadn't hurt her, but was unable to think much past that. My cock finished engorging, the bulbous base filling with blood. She gasped as it did so, and I whined as I felt my flesh clasped within hers. Bliss! For a moment, I thought I was dying, my heart pounding within my chest, the whole of my sensation emanating from my loins. I was hardly aware of the tender flesh of my underbelly touching her back and buttocks, the contact feeling both distant and unreal and intimate, as though it were a part of me. I whined incoherently as I felt the tension build within me, listening to her gasps and grunts with growing ecstasy. I felt the familiar tightness in my spine and pelvis; my hips were humping spastically, and I knew I was close to coming.

With a groan of happiness, she pushed herself against me, her ass wiggling beneath me. Our motions combined, increased, and I felt an incredible rush of bliss directly up the center of my body, a white-hot current burning into my brain. My flesh was fully expanded within hers, and my body had taken over, all thought erased.

I yelped happily, her groans and cries a counterpoint to my excitement as I moved to extricate myself from above her.

She was still screaming and writhing beneath me as I lifted my left foreleg and placed it on her right side along with my other foreleg, each movement causing explosions of pleasure from my swollen cock, eliciting pained-sounding grunts from her. I gave a tremendous exertion and with a small hop I managed to step all the way over her ass, my final position facing opposite her, our rear ends together. In retrospect, I am grateful that my consciousness was eclipsed shortly thereafter; the thought of getting hung up with Samantha, connected by the genitals, in the middle of the woods, was more than my vanity can bear.

Once I was facing in the opposite direction an enormous amount of traction was placed on my cock, my hips going like gentle clockwork, barely moving. I began ejaculating, my penis pulsing as jets of semen entered her body from mine. I was coming. . . . My spine reacted as though a ball of white light had formed at its base. . . . It crept quickly upward, a fluid pulsation of life. . . . It hit my . . . brain. . . . Ahhhhhh. . . . Bliss. . . . My consciousness dissolved, once and for all . . . in her . . . in her body. . . . I was dying, my mind blissful. . . . I was . . . dissolving . . . in . . . her . . . body. . . . I . . . was . . . We. . . . Her. . . . One. . . . God. . . .

I regained myself about half an hour later, sprawled on top of her, our bodies lathed with sweat.

Sam.

I feared I had hurt her until she opened her eyes and smiled, kissed me. Then it all came back to me . . . Where I was, what we had done.

"Sam," I croaked, realizing I had reverted to human shape. We kissed again, properly this time, now that I was so equipped.

"Love," she whispered.

"Love," I answered.

I wanted to lay there on top of her forever. She had turned over beneath me, dislodging my limp penis and leaving a huge puddle of wetness beneath and between us. She grinned as I grimaced.

"Sorry," I muttered.

"Nothing to be sorry about," she said in a sincere voice, running her hand across my naked, relatively hairless chest. "It's the way you're designed. Just re-mind me . . ." She brushed a strand of hair from her sweaty face, and I noticed that patches of hair I had shed as I reverted clung to her sweaty body. ". . . never to let you con me into giving you head." I couldn't help laughing.

"Yes," I agreed, feeling better already. "I'll keep that in mind."

"A question, dear Jack," she said, as I sorted her clothes from mine. "Did you actually come all that time?" She paused, "I mean, I know you came, but did you, climax? Did you—"

"You mean, since I ejaculated for almost the whole time, you were wondering if I was also climaxing the whole time, right?" I interpreted for her. She nodded, biting her lower lip, something she did when she was curious. "And the answer," I said, shifting unsteadily on my feet, "is yes." Her eyes widened.

"God," she said, appreciatively. "And you're *embarrassed* about this? Most men would be screaming it from the rooftops." She shook her head and stood up, still exuding fluid. I noticed she was none too steady on her feet either, her quadriceps entertaining quick spasms up and down their lengths. "I came the whole time, too," she said, as she stretched, sounding very self-satisfied. I helped her into her clothes.

"You've got to be freezing," I said. She nodded, her teeth chattering for the first time.

"Now that you mention it," she said, laughing and shivering at the same time. After she finished dressing, I began donning my own clothes.

"Zip that coat," I said. "You've probably caught your death of cold out here."

"Actually, no." She shook her head. "I wasn't cold at all while we made love. Your hair," she paused, plucking several strands of my hair from where they clung to her neck, "is a remarkable insulator." I rolled my eyes and she zipped her coat. We headed back to the car, leaving the blood-streaked bones where they lay.

"Jack," she said, as I slid my arm around her waist. "I love you." I kissed her on the cheek.

"I love you, too," I said, knowing it was true.

VALENTINE'S DAY IN JAIL

Susan Musgrave

Western wind when will thou blow?
The small rain down can rain.
Christ that my love were in my arms
And I in my bed again.
ANON.

The bus dropped me in the heart of town, across from the funeral parlor, where a sign in the window read, "Closed for the Season."

"No one dies much this time of year?" I asked, making small talk with the taxi driver taking me the rest of the way to the prison. "Not if they do it around here," he replied, and then asked me if I minded if he smoked.

Before I could answer, he lit one and blew the smoke out his window. I sat in the back watching rain streak the windshield as he talked about the justice system and how "sickos like drug dealers" should be shot to save taxpayers' money. He must have thought I worked at the prison because he kept glancing in the rearview mirror, waiting for me to agree. I explained I was visiting a convicted marijuana smuggler, a Colombian, doing life, that it might even be love. He apologized, saying he should have kept his trap shut. He said there must be one heck of a lucky guy waiting for me inside, that all he'd ever wanted was a soft girl in his bed every night, and all he'd ever been was disappointed.

I looked away into the mountains above the distant town of Hope, the snowy ridges few had ever set foot on, and tried to picture what Angel, the lucky man, might be doing at this moment. I imagined him lying on his bunk, staring up at the dull green institutional gloss on his ceiling, with not even a crack or a ridge he could use as landmarks.

"So when's the honeymoon?" the driver pressed. The window had steamed up, and he wiped a little space with his hand. "You going to escape? Go someplace tropical? Swimming pool, palm trees, hula-hula. You wish, huh?"

We rounded a bend at the northern end of the valley, and Toombs Penitentiary came into view. All that separated it from its sister prison, Toombs Penitentiary for Women, was the Corrections Mountain View Cemetery. Both prisons were cut off from the world by mountains so high their western flanks were always in shadow.

I'd met Angel when I visited both prisons, and the adjoining cemetery, a year ago. I had just begun freelancing and hoped to cover the story behind the high rate of inmate suicides over Christmas. "No one but the law ever wanted them when they were alive, and now

no one wants them," an official told me, indicating the
forlorn tract of land, overgrown with scagweed, where
the unclaimed bodies of lifers were laid to rest. Escape
risks, he told me, were even buried in leg irons.

My driver let me off in the parking lot, a hundred
yards from the front gate, and wished me luck. "You
know, you make me jealous," he said. "You get to go in
there and be all lovey-dovey while I go back to work." I
paid him and stood for a moment watching him drive
away, then turned to face the prison.

The heavy gold watch on my wrist told me it was
12:45, and I had to stand outside in the rain, waiting,
until the big hand on the clock inside gave its single
digit salute to the sky. Then the guard buzzed me in. I
waited some more as he went through my handbag,
taking apart my fountain pen and getting ink all over
his hands. I was allowed to take in with me a tube of
mascara and lipstick, but not the lozenges that Xaviera
Hollander, the *Penthouse* columnist, had recommended
as a prelude to oral sex.

"Leave these in there," he said, pointing me toward a
metal locker. "And this, too." He held up the loose tampon he'd found at the bottom of my bag. "Security mea-
sure," he said. "An inmate could suicide himself by
choking on one."

He repacked my handbag, saying they would supply
me with a substitute if I needed it. "The matron will see
you next," he said, pointing to a door marked NO EXIT.
On the other side of the door I could hear a woman
protesting.

I sat on a hard chair and waited. Angel's sister
emerged, with the red-faced matron, Miss Horis, behind her. Consuelo, which was her current alias, had

told me to trust her—she could hide *anything*. Why wouldn't I trust a woman who had smuggled herself and three kilos of cocaine into the country so she could pay her brother's legal fees, and be near him? Angel told me, too, she had once smuggled a grenade in her vagina into Bella Vista prison in Colombia. The condom she'd offered to carry for me today seemed like small beer in comparison.

"Miserable enough out there for you?" Miss Horis asked, sighing as she ushered me into the NO EXIT room, then telling me to remove my coat, suit, blouse, under-things, and "all other personal items." Naked, I placed both feet firmly in the middle of the mirror.

"Straddle the mirror, please, one foot on either side. That's it. Now relax, and cough twice."

I coughed, and Miss Horis peered in the mirror, then asked me to lift my breasts one at a time, before open-ing my mouth where she checked under my tongue. "Enjoy Valentine's Day," she said, as she left me to get dressed again.

She hadn't mentioned the watch—obviously meant for a man's wrist. I got dressed again and she popped her head in the door a moment later, offering me a sani-tary napkin to replace the seized tampon. I shook my head no. No inmate, evidently, had yet thought of try-ing to suffocate himself with a Kotex.

Once inside the Visiting Room I headed for the wash-room, where I found Consuelo fighting with her hair. A sign informing visitors that there was "No Necking, Petting, Fondling, Embracing, Tickling, Slapping, Pinching, or Biting Permitted During Visits" was posted above the condom machine (foreplay might be prohibited, the machine's presence seemed to suggest, but fucking was not). Today the machine bore another warning: "Sorry. Out of Order." The word "Sorry" had been crossed out.

I turned to Consuelo for the condom she was supposed to smuggle in for me, but she held out her empty hands. "I had to swallow it," she said. "That woman she wanted to look me in the mouth." She said Angel and I should get married so we would be approved for private visits. But Angel and I weren't waiting for approval. Today our names were at the top of a clandestine list for a different kind of private visit—the unsanctioned kind. I borrowed Consuelo's comb and dragged it through my own damp tangles.

At half-past one, Mr. Saygrover, the Visitors and Communications officer, led us into a hallway painted the same avocado green as the outside of the prison. He nodded to the young guard in control of the first of the iron-barred gates blocking our passageway, and the heavy steel doors parted on their runners. We crossed five more identical barriers before reaching the gymnasium.

I could see the men pressed up against the last gate, awaiting their visitors. All were dressed in green shirts and pressed trousers the same shade as the prison walls. The ritual had been the same ever since I first started visiting Angel—the men standing behind the barrier waiting and waving, and the women approaching, awkwardly, looking at one another for reassurance, like girls at a junior high "turnabout" sockhop. The closer we got, the longer it seemed to take the guards to open the barriers. A female guard with sweat stains in the armpits of her uniform opened the last gate. Janis Joplin's voice came rasping out of two coffin-sized speakers strapped high on the gymnasium wall. She didn't need to tell anyone here how freedom was only another word for nothing left to lose.

The gym was decorated with red balloons and white streamers. The streamers had been affixed from corner to corner the night before and had lost their elasticity. A prison sculptor's papier-mâché heart, trapped in barbed wire, lay on display next to the Coke machine, which was also "Out of Order."

Visitors found seats around the long banquet tables, each one laden with the institution's version of hors d'oeuvres: mini-sizzlers on toothpicks, rolled cold cuts, radishes that had been sculpted to look like roses too terrified to open, a pyramid of mystery-meat sandwiches and plates of heart-shaped cookies baked by prisoners in the kitchen. My eyes moved from table to table, searching. Angel sat upright on a metal chair, arms folded across his chest. Our eyes locked. He stood up.

Nothing had changed. He didn't speak. I couldn't. He had a smile bittersweet as a pill for the sick at heart, a pair of lips you wanted to lick under a mustache that would keep you from getting close enough, and sad night eyes. His hair was straight and black and today he wore it tied back in a ponytail. In my last letter I'd written, "Tie your hair back so it won't get in the way. I want to see my juice all over your face."

Angel pulled two chairs together so we could sit facing one another, and he leaned forward and put both his arms around my neck. "I'm always afraid I'll never see you again, that you won't come back," he said, breaking the silence. "I'm afraid you might find me—too available."

I laughed as I cupped his dark face in my hands. "I

wouldn't call any man doing life behind bars *too avail-able*." His mustache, smelling of the red-hot cinnamon hearts he sucked every time I visited to hide the smell of the dark tobacco on his breath, scoured my upper lip. More than his smile or his eyes, I think it was his smell that attracted me most the first time we met, like the air before a storm, long before there is any visible sign of it.

"You look thin," I said, sitting back in my chair. "Are you getting everything you need?" Angel sat back, too, straightening the sheet that served as a tablecloth. He picked up an orange and poked his finger into its navel.

"I'm getting your letters every day. And you're here. What more do I need?" He kissed me, but I pulled away. "And you?" he asked.

I needed privacy. I wanted to be with Angel, alone. We'd had one chance, at the Christmas social, to spend five minutes in the toilet stall of the men's lavatory, but I needed more time than that to fondle him, embrace, tickle, neck, pet, slap, pinch, and bite—it was all I had thought about since we'd met. I pictured him alone every night in his cell, penis erect and shining, sad as tinsel at an unattended party. When we were together, I was aware of how close he stayed beside me and how every time we brushed against one another I felt a shiver of something long lost stirring inside me, the same longing I'd felt for a brown-eyed boy in the fifth grade, my last painful crush before the crash of puberty.

I'd been afraid, too, I told Angel, afraid I had "gone too far." In my last letter I'd quoted Kurt Vonnegut, who said the only task remaining for a writer in the twenti-eth century was to describe a blow-job artistically. I told Angel I'd rather *show* him a blow-job than write about it, then went on to discuss the calorie count in a mouth-

ful of sperm (one swallow contained thirty-two different chemicals, including vitamin C, vitamin B12, fruc-
tose, sulphur, zinc, copper, potassium, calcium, and
other healthy things). I said I had a One-a-Day Multiple
Vitamin habit but figured I could give these up if he
were willing to have oral sex once a day.

Angel told me "far" was the only place worth going,
and he kissed me again. This time I didn't stop him. He
shifted on the hard chair, adjusting the bulge that
strained to break out of his trousers. I squirmed on the
warm metal, forcing my knees together, my sex swollen,
struggling to escape. I caught two guards staring at us; I
nudged Angel and we pushed back from one another.
Angel held my hand underneath the table, stroking it
with his thumb. "I haven't been in the yard yet today,"
he said, after a silence. We'd been having the same
thought. Out there we might be alone. "How is it, outside? The weather?"

"Wet," I said, taking a heart-shaped cookie and
breaking it in half. Angel took the other half from my
hands, and I watched it shrink under his mustache.
"Raining."

"Good," he said. "Let's walk."

We had the yard to ourselves, almost. Two guards in a
patrol vehicle slowed to look us over as we stopped to
watch a pregnant doe browsing on the thick grasses
outside the perimeter fence. It was the same spot, Angel
said, where a half-blind bear had been shot in the autumn. Angel said the guards had fired warning shots at
her, but she kept coming back. A handful of yellow-
and-purple cartridge shells lay in the wet grass.

"She couldn't see well enough to get away while she
had a chance?" I asked.

"Few see that well," said Angel, and when he looked at me this time I saw, in the gleam of his shadowy eyes, a depth of wanting that promised heaven.

We kept to a well-worn trail Angel called the warning track. Walking, we lifted our faces to scale the double high-wire fences but stayed well inside the dead line, the line beyond which any prisoner would be shot. Angel pointed to where a man had been picked off by the tower guard "before his hands were even bloodied by the razor wire."

I squinted up through the rain, beyond the gun towers, to the sky. Angel slid his hand in under my thin coat, cupping my breasts, milking my nipples between his thumb and forefinger, and I felt the wet silk of my panties sticking to me where I was open, and a thin seam of silk rubbing back and forth across my clitoris with every step. But Angel, his faraway eyes on the towers, seemed to have scaled the high-wire fences and left me behind. Then, as we rounded a bend in the warning track, he said someday he would take me so high, so far up in the Andes, nobody, not even God, could stare down at us.

"You're dreaming." I screwed up my face at him. I didn't need to say it out loud: "You're stuck in here doing life." Angel knew my thinking.

"Life can be shorter than you expect," he said. Then he looked at me and laughed, in a way.

I laughed, too, but pulled him closer. For now this was good enough.

When the call came over the loudspeaker to clear the yard we went back inside, elbowing our way through a cluster of guards who'd been checking us out from the door. We sat in our wet clothes holding each other and waiting as more guards pinned two sheets together to make a screen on the gymnasium wall. The Inmate Committee had planned to show *Carmen* before the food was served. Angel whispered what he wanted me to do when the lights dimmed, but now, without the condom for protection, and surveillance from every corner of the room, my heart started looking for an emergency exit. I told Angel we had too much to lose, including our visits. But then the lights went down, he lifted the hem of the tablecloth with his foot, and pushed me under.

Beneath the table, in a private world, I sat hugging my knees, feeling lost and uncomfortable. The Inmate Committee, in charge of all forms of entertainment, had transformed the space under the table into a low-ceilinged motel room. We had a foam mattress, two arsenic-green blankets, and a pillow, upon which someone had placed a long-stemmed rose. My mouth felt dry. How was I going to give Angel that blow-job? I longed for those lozenges and thought about the editor from *Elle* who'd phoned a few months ago asking for reminiscences of "my most embarrassing sexual encounter" for their Valentine's Day issue. I'd been unable to come up with anything, but now, as I sat composing the story in my head, I concluded a guard must have seen me and apprehended Angel. I would be forced to wait it out under the table until such time as they chose to humiliate me publicly; precisely the ending I needed for my date from hell for *Elle.*

I felt a hand go over my eyes, then (the smell of him!) Angel began kissing me all over my face and head, sniffing my hair along the part line. When he took his hands away from my eyes I saw he was wearing dry clothes.

"I went back to my house to change," he said, laughing, taking off his jacket and draping it over my shoulders. "Your dress is soaked," he said. "Wear this, too." He began to unbutton his shirt.

He peeled back the blanket, gave me his dry shirt, and made me get under the covers. I told him he was the first man I'd been to bed with who tried to make me put more clothes *on*, and he told me I was the first woman who could make him hard and make him laugh at the same time. He wanted to know if all Canadian women could do that, and I said as far as I knew there'd never been a poll.

We kept our voices low. The room, too, grew quiet, as the credits began to roll. "Are you sure this is safe?" I whispered. "What if a guard saw us?"

"No one saw us," he said, as he pulled off his undershirt. For the first time I saw the hollow place in his chest. It looked as if his heart had been excavated, like the ruin I once visited in the remote Yucatán. Everything of value had been dug out and taken away. Only a pit remained, which, over the years, had been reclaimed by the jungle.

"I was born with this . . ." He took my hand, curled it into a fist, and placed it in the little hollow. "My mother used to say by the time I died it would have filled up with the tears she would shed for me during her lifetime."

I laid my head on the pillow, waiting for the table to be pulled out from over us. It took an effort of love to get in the mood, staring up at the words PROPERTY OF

CORRECTIONS CANADA MORGUE stamped on the underside of the table. I shut my eyes tight as Angel picked apart the rose, then laid the cool crimson petals on my eyelids.

"You're not like any woman I've ever known," he said, pressing his nose in my armpit and edging one finger under the elastic of my bra.

"What's that like?" I shook the petals away.

"Uuuummmmmmmmm," was all he said. I wanted to undo his zipper and take his cock in my mouth, but something made me hold back, an old memory, perhaps, of my first "most embarrassing date" in the old boathouse smelling of high tide, fish, and water rats. I was twelve and Dick Wolfe (not his real name, but close) showed me how to set a banana slug on fire, how it would melt into a pool of sticky stuff if you had the right touch. Then he undid his pants, and I remember it looked so eager, so trusting, as he said, "Put your mouth on it," and when he came I thought I'd cut him with my tooth, the crooked one my parents could never afford to have fixed. I believed I had a mouthful of his blood but did the polite thing, I thought, and swallowed it. "I've cut you," I said, thinking we'd have to go to the hospital and how was I going to explain cutting a boy "down there"? Then he said, his brown eyes more open to me than ever, "That wasn't blood, sweetheart."

"It's been a long time," Angel said, as I lay still, dreaming, half-listening to someone at our table tuning a guitar. My arm was going to sleep, and I shifted position. The movie had begun, and the man who'd been tuning his guitar began strumming on it so passionately that Angel and I could no longer talk. Then the projector shut down and the lights went back on. The voices up above us grew louder, as if an argument were taking place.

"Something's up," said Angel. "It sounds like there's a problem with the projector."

"The lights have come on," I said. "How are we going to get out of here without someone seeing us? What sort of person will they think I am?"

"No one is going to blame you," Angel said. "The guards will just think I corrupted you. They think all inmates are criminals."

He put his arms around me as if to reassure me. Then he saw the watch I was wearing and asked if it was a gift. He didn't say "from another man," but I could hear it in his question. I unstrapped it from my wrist and said yes, a gift for him. It was guaranteed to be shockproof and never to lose time.

"I've never owned a watch that didn't break down," he said. "I think watches get nervous being on my wrist."

I pushed him back so I could move my pillow away from the end of the table, where a pair of knees was invading our love nest.

"This one comes with a lifetime warranty," I said.

Angel settled his body back alongside mine and blew a strand of hair out of my face. He shifted again so his chin rested on my shoulder blade. The person with the intruding knees began tapping his feet and calling for more music.

It was growing stuffier under the table, and neither of us had enough legroom. But I'd waited long enough: I slipped my arms out of my dress, pulled him close to me, and kissed him, for a long time. It didn't matter that up above us there was a world of men and women arguing and laughing. (The film, I learned, leaving the social, had turned out to be *Carne,* sadomasochistic pornography, not *Carmen* the opera, and the guards axed the show.) We were alone in the new world of our flesh, and the occasional appearance of the toe of a running shoe under the hem of the tablecloth, or a hand slapping the tabletop, no longer felt like an intrusion.

"But will you still respect me after this?" I smiled.

He took my hand and guided it to his cock. "My respect for you knows no limits."

I unzipped his trousers. Erotic texts from ancient India claim there is a definite relationship between the size of an erect penis and the destiny of its owner. The possessors of thin penises would be very lucky, those with long ones were fated to be poor, those with short ones could become rulers of the land, and males with thick penises were doomed always to be unhappy.

For now, I was destined to make Angel happy. I began licking the end of his cock, which was already swollen. I thought it was going to burst as my tongue busied itself.

"I'm going to die," he said. When I looked up at his face, across the nut-brown expanse of his body, he smiled back, that slow smile, and I took his cock in both my hands. I could barely get my fingers around it. Its head had a ruddy glow and was grinning. It glistened. I kissed it. Sniffed it. Sucked it hard, taking as much of it into my mouth as I could, then licking it again, making a lot of noise while I sucked and licked.

"I'll come if you keep doing that," he said.

Then he pulled me up so I lay next to him and reached inside my panties. He said my cunt nuzzled up to his hand like a horse's soft mouth when you feed it sugar. He moved down between my legs, pulling my panties aside, sliding one finger inside me, sliding it out, sliding two fingers in, then sliding them out, then sliding three fingers in. I arched my back, spreading my legs wider to give him better access, and he tugged gently upward on my pubic hair, baring my clitoris. Then he began licking me, slowly, teasingly, moving in small circles with his lips and tongue, his kisses falling on me, gentle as the scent of rain in a lemon grove. My body strained against his face, and when he looked up at me, his skin was alive with my juices.

I sat up and pulled him down on top of me.

"I don't have any protection," he said.

There are some exquisite moments from which we are not meant to be protected. I slid him inside me, achingly. I had never had anything so hard inside me. I held my breath as he kept coming into me, we were breathing and then not breathing in unison, and I brought his hand up to my mouth to cover it, suppress any sound, and then I began sucking his fingers, one at a time, then two at a time, then three. His fingers tasted of salt, of my own sweat, and juices. "Suck," he said, and pushed into me, harder still, as if by trying he could disappear up inside me and escape forever into the rich orchid darkness of my womb. When he came his face became contorted as if it hurt him to come so hard, then we lay quietly for a while, and then he began licking me again, making me come with his own come, with his tongue, his lips, and his fingertips. I cried when I came, and doubled up, curling into myself. He began kissing me, from my toes up along my legs and the insides of my thighs, over my belly and breasts, up my neck and onto my face and in my hair. He said this was his way of kissing me hello and good-bye at the same time.

Afterward as I lay on a bed of bruised rose petals, licking the drops of sweat that had rolled down his chest and collected in the hollow above his heart, Angel said coming inside me was like coming on velvet rails. And later when we'd crawled out from under the table and were standing alone once more in the slanting rain, we kissed again. We kissed as if to seal our fate, to finish a life together we hadn't even begun.

Years ago, on an island in the tropics, I had been lured from my bed in the night by the air pregnant with the scent of vanilla. I found giant cauldron-like cactus flowers opening in the moonlight and thousands of tiny sphinx moths fluttering from one pod to another. In the morning, when I came to show them to a friend, the flowers had disappeared.

I missed the next visit because I had a deadline to meet (a piece about these cactus flowers that bloom one night a year, conduct their whole sex lives, and vanish by dawn) and the one after that because the prison was locked down. There'd been a stabbing, and a hostage-taking, and rumblings of a hunger strike. I wrote to Angel, concerned about his health. He wrote back, worried about mine. He hoped I wasn't pregnant, for though he liked the idea—that way part of him had already escaped for good—he didn't want to leave me with a burden.

Angel must have sensed it: Visits weren't the only thing I'd missed that month. I made a doctor's appointment. In the evening I tried to phone Angel, but good news was not enough of a reason to bring an inmate to the phone. I asked to book a Special Visit to see him the

BEST AMERICAN EROTICA 1995

next day. An officer informed me that Special Visits were granted for death or bereavement only. So I had to save my news until I could sit across from Angel in the Visiting Room and touch his face, let him take my hand under the table and stroke it with his thumb.

But the next time I saw Angel, he was in the news. "Two men are dead after today's daring escape attempt from Toombs Penitentiary," was all I heard; my heart began to pound to the staccato beat of a police helicopter, a throaty thwap thwap thwapping. I moved closer to the screen and turned up the sound. "Earlier this afternoon two Colombian nationals tried to climb aboard a waiting helicopter that had landed in the prison yard . . ." There was a shot of the dead line where Angel and I had walked, then a file-photo closeup of his face.

"Life can be shorter than you expect." Consuelo and I rode the bus to the prison in the rain. She said Angel hadn't confided in me, hadn't been able to tell me about his escape plan, out of respect . . . *my respect for you knows no limits* . . . but that he'd been insistent: He would send for me when it was safe. My good news— that I wasn't pregnant—seemed like sad news now. All of him had escaped for good.

Mr. Saygrover asked Consuelo to sign for Angel's property, which fit in a gray plastic suitcase. Consuelo looked inside, then handed it to me. Angel, she said, would have wanted me to have everything. He had left his battered *Pocket Oxford*, a key chain with no keys, a toothbrush, an unopened bag of Cheetos, and $2.37 in change. And, he had left me. So much for respect!

A service took place in the prison chapel. A handful of fellow inmates gathered to pay their last respects, the chaplain mumbled a few words and asked us to pray.

Consuelo said Angel wouldn't have wanted hymns, so she sang a song from their childhood, "*Si me han de matar mañana, que me maten de una vez*": "If they're going to kill me tomorrow, they might as well kill me right now."

I wanted, for a moment, to kill him, myself, all over again, until I saw him lying that still in his gray Styrofoam coffin. I tried to hold one of his hands—awkward because of the handcuffs—then stroked one of his thumbs instead. He wore the watch. I could hear it ticking.

I moved my hands down over his body, saying hello to Angel, saying good-bye. And when I felt the leg irons at his ankles, I wanted to rip open his shirt and let my tears collect in the hollow place in his chest.

But I didn't weep. Through the bars of the chapel window I watched the slow rain falling on the fake-fur trim of the guards' brown jackets, and thought how lonely it would be, how cold and cramped the earth Angel was going into. In this world, I knew, there was an unending supply of sorrow, and the heart could always make room for more.

CINNAMON ROSES

Renee M. Charles

I DON'T KNOW if it's because people buy so heavily into the mythos of vampirism (y'know, the gal/guy-in-a-sweeping-cape-swooping-down-on-her/his-prey's lily-white, blue-veined throat batcrap), or if it's because they have this idea that we vampires just need a suck of blood every day or so to keep body and soul in one just slightly undead package, but being a twentieth-century working vampire is *not* just a matter of staking out a little patch of earth under an abandoned warehouse somewhere out in the hinterlands of the city—c'mon, get real.

Spending twelve or more hours a night biting and swooping and not much else is fucking *boring*. And it doesn't contribute squat toward the rent or utilities on my basement apartment in Greenwich Village, either.

Besides, just because a gal gets a little more than she bargained for during an admittedly dumb unsafest-sex-of-all fling with some guy she met in some club she can't even remember the name of (oh, I made him wear a condom, but that didn't protect my neck . . .) it doesn't mean that she suddenly becomes the reincarnation of Dracula's Brides. I still needed to make a living, and since I'd been a barber/hairstylist before . . . well, you've got to admit, scissors and razors do have a way of occasionally drawing blood.

And from personal experience, I know that vampire bites feel a heck of a lot like the touch of a styptic pencil . . . down to the not-quite-needle-sharp tip pressing down on warm flesh.

Getting my boss to let me change my hours from mid-afternoon to evening to evening to pre-dawn wasn't difficult; the place where I work, the Heads-or-Tails, is one of those places that specializes in punk/SM/adventuresome types—full body waxes, razor and lather shaves, even a little extra stuff on the side (regular customers only—cop shops can't afford to send in decoys week after week) so it isn't unusual to see just about every type of person coming in for that special cut or shave at any hour of the night.

And at one hundred bucks a pop and up per session, the Heads-or-Tails never closes. So when one of the stylists demands a *right now* change in working hours, the management is more than happy to oblige, especially when she (as in me) keeps drawing repeat nocturnal customers. . . .

Another misconception about us vampires is that if we keep on doing what we do best—a.k.a. neck-biting and blood-sucking—eventually we'll infect the entire fucking world, because our victims will infect victims of their own, and so on until you're looking at one of those

Andy Warhol's *Dracula* situations (the whiny vampire strapping his coffin on top of the touring car and motoring off in search of fresh "wurgin" blood). Get off it, do you think that one sip from a person is enough to make them go mirror invisible (which is another load of bullsheet—sorry, but the laws of physics don't work that way, though it makes for a nice special effect in the movies, I'll admit!) and start draining the family dog for a pre-bedtime snack? I had to spend a week with my nightclub Nosferatu before sunlight began to make my skin itch, but I can still put on my lipstick in the mirror, thank you!

So, a slip of the disposable razor here, or a nick with the scissors there, and it's good-bye hunger, but not necessarily hello fellow night-walker. Not unless *I'm* interested in some continuing companionship over the course of a month or so. And even then, I make sure I know the potential victim well enough to be sure that she or he will be in a position to tap into a private food supply without attracting attention. C'mon, do you think that some of those E.R. nurses on the graveyard shift keep missing your veins by accident? Or those dental technicians who can't seem to clean your teeth without drawing blood?

But sometimes, no matter how much a gal exercises caution, and forethought, not to mention common sense, there will come the day when that certain customer walks in—and every vein in my body, every blood-seeks-blood-filled throbbing vein, cries out to my brain, my lips, my cunt: *Take this one . . . don't ask any questions, don't think about the night after . . . just take this one.*

(Doesn't even matter if *this one* is a gal or a guy; skin

touching skin is gratification enough, and fingers and tongues more than equal a prick. . . . There's nerve endings enough to go around all over the body).

For me, the first signal of a customer being a *taker* is their smell. The smell of clean, healthy blood surging under their veins just a few millimeters under the unbroken flesh—for each of us, the name, the associative taste, we give to that good blood-odor differs. For me, it's cinnamon; cinnamon that's been freshly scraped from the stick, that raw, so-sharp-it-tweaks-your-nostrils tang, so fresh and unseasoned the smell soon becomes a palatable taste even before the first drop caresses my tongue.

(How else do you think vampires avoid HIV and AIDS? Once you've had a whiff of that moldy-grapes and stale-bread odor—naturally, this perception differs from vampire to vampire—you can smell a victim coming at you from two blocks away. Three if the wind is blowing past them.)

Oh, all non-infected normals smell somewhat like cinnamon to me now; as long as you're reasonably healthy, the cinnamon-tang is there, but in some people . . . well, it's more like a cautious sprinkle of the spice over toast, or across the top of an unsealed apple pie. Maybe it's all the *stuff* people take; additives, drugs, you name it. But in a taker, that fragrance is a living part of them, like an extra finger or breast. Richer and more lingering than the smell of sex, more piquant than ejaculation seeping out of your crevices.

But the blood isn't the whole reason for that desire to own, to make a normal into a new-blood kin; even though it is the most tangible reason; for me (at least), there has to be a certain look in their eyes, a vulnerability that goes deeper than mere submission. The look which says *What I am now is not all I could be.* Doesn't matter if the look comes from eyes in a straight or gay or female or male body, either. Like I said before, there's nerve ends aplenty all over the body. Age isn't a biggie either, although most of the clientele of the H.-or-T. is youngish, adventuresome.

Color, background, whatever—none of those things matter either. Maybe because we vampires live so much in ourselves, and are ruled by what runs through our bodies and not over our bodies, that which is within others speaks to us so eloquently, so desperately.

Even if they themselves do not realize that inner need. . . .

Despite the air conditioning in my private cubicle (set on 72° instead of something cooler—newly shorn flesh, especially large areas of it, does tend to chill easily), the muggy heat of the late July night managed to seep into my workspace that particular evening, and I was just about to slip off my panties and position myself directly in front of the unit for a few moments when that smell hit my nostrils. *Taker coming.* I quickly lowered my suede skirt and smoothed down the short-cropped hair which covered my head like a sleek skullcap, before glancing about my workspace to make sure everything was in perfect, customer-ready order. Unopened bags of flexible-blade razors—check. Cleaned and oiled clippers, trimmers, edgers—check. Shave creams, mug soaps, depilatories—check. Thin rubber gloves—not that I really needed them, but Health Department regulations are regulations—check. Hot wax—check.

By this time, I could hear footsteps coming closer

down the narrow tile hallway between workstations. This one's a woman, my brain told my body. My labia began to do a jerking, twitching dance against the already damp fabric of my panties, but I made my other set of lips form themselves into that slightly vacant, blandly professional smile all of my customers got when they parted the thick curtains separating my cubicle from all the others in the H.-or-T. salon.

In deference to the heat without, she was wearing a halter top, shorts, and slip-on cotton-topped shoes, the kind the Chinese make by the thousands in an hour or so. Can't rightly say I remember what color any of her clothes were; but *her* colors . . . well, you know how it is when you see your first really brilliant sunrise, don't you? (Even though those are forbidden to my kind, the memories—the skills, and the like to need to go on surviving—remain.)

Within, she was a molten cinnamon, and without, she was a sunrise, or a sunset . . . whichever is the most vivid, the most heart-aching. Russet hair flecked with streaks of natural gold and near-orange fell across her forehead and shoulders like lava arrested by a sudden chill, while her eyebrows were twin arcing bird wings above green-like-gumdrops and suck-it-till-your-mouth-puckers hard candies, or new leaves in the sunlight I could no longer see—green, green eyes. And she had the type of skin that let that cinnamon-scraped-from-the-stick lifeblood of hers shine through in delicate vine-looping trails of palest filtered blue and labia pink. Real redhead skin. And I don't know why it is, but so many true redheads like her are so naturally thin, not to the point of bones sticking out, but covered with just enough flesh. Breasts small enough to cup in a woman's palm, but the nipples would be big and hard enough to make an imprint on that same smallish palm.

It was painful not to be able to drink her in for as long as I wished; but staring at the customers, especially new ones (and most especially takers) can sometimes send them turning on their heels and diving through those heavy curtains, never to be seen or smelled again. Fortunately for me, she was nervous enough not to notice that I was staring at, no, *devouring* her, for her green-beyond-green eyes were timidly lowered, darting to a picture she held in her left hand, then back at a point right around my waistline. She probably didn't even realize I was doing the looking.

Which suited me just fine.

I could see the picture she was holding; a newspaper clipping of that one model, the French-Canadian one with the dragon tattooed on her shorn scalp. Well, at least it wasn't Susan Powter; I'd have been loathe to try and bleach that exquisite liquid cinnamon hair of hers.

"Uhm, the woman up front said you do . . . what'd she call it? 'Full-head shaves?' "

Customer or not, taker or not, I felt a sharp pang when she said that—not at all unlike the first time my lounge-lizard Lothario sank his incisors into my neck. Even if it meant being so close to her exposed neck, shearing off that mane wouldn't give me the usual pleasure I felt as my labia quivered in time with the buzzing hum of the heavy-duty clippers which would send my hand and arm to quivering as I'd take off the longest layer of hair. Usually, shearing off hair could be a sensual, aesthetic experience above and beyond the sight of those subcutaneous veins resting in the flesh of the newly exposed neck; the way it rippled as it fell away from the scalp, drifting down in feathery piles to the floor, sometimes thick swaths of it touching my bare legs on the way down, tickling like a man's hairy leg brushing against my own, or the way light picked up the sheen of untanned, milky skin under the quarter-inch stubble, and as the lather was swept away by each pull of the blade, the play of diffuse light on naked flesh and the silky feel of it through the thin rubber gloves were usually enough to give me an orgasm on the spot.

Then again, most of my customers had average, unre-markable hair. Being obvious about my potential plea-sure would've driven her away before I'd come even within tasting distance of her exposed flesh and spice-laden veins, so I smiled more naturally and replied, "That's my speciality. . . . I can do either lather shaves, or just clipper—"

Somewhat reluctantly, the taker replied, "No, not just clippered . . . my boyfriend, he has this thing about skin, y'know . . . all over."

The words "my boyfriend" were an explanation—and a challenge. Most of my female customers went for the Powter or O'Connor look because their lovers were spending too much time ogling those chrome-pated, unattainable TV visions, and judging by how few of them returned for touch-ups, either their boyfriend took over the daily shaving chore, or they realized that wear-ing a wig on the job was a consummate drag (the salon also sold wigs on the side), and went back to doing the hair-spread-over-the-pillow thing, and to hell with what Boyfriend thought. But there was always the possibility that Boyfriend might like an entirely naked girl, too, so as casually as possible, I assured her, "I'll do a close job, so your boyfriend should be pleased. . . . You said 'all over,' didn't you? As in—"

At that she blushed; the rush of blood coming to her cheeks made my mouth water and my labia jerk so hard I had to (albeit casually) cross my legs as I leaned back against the countertop behind me. Reaching up to toy with a thick curl of hair for what might be the last time in a long time—depending on how pleased Boyfriend was with my efforts—she licked her lips and said softly, "I was embarrassed to ask out front, but I figured since there's the word 'Tails' in the name of the shop . . . he'd like it . . . y'know, down there, too. He said he'd like to be able to—" at this she blushed deeper, until the reddish glow seeped into her makeup free eyelids " '—see the rose as he's plucking it.' I know it sounds weird, but . . . well, he's given me a lot of flowers, on my birthday and on our anniversary of when we met and all, all of them these pink bud roses . . . and what he has the florists write on the cards can be a little, y'know, embarrassing, especially when they deliver the flowers to the bank where I work, but . . . you know. It's not like it's real cool to send a guy a rose in a bud vase. . . ."

Her words took me back to my first few nights with the one who took *me* into this world, the same world I was aching to bring her into with a few styptic-stinging kisses. I'd been spread open before him on his bed, a pillow placed beneath my behind, and he'd been tracing the contours of my glistening pinkness with a lazy forefinger, telling me, "Do you ever look at yourself, opened like this, in a mirror? I thought so. . . . Have you noticed, how each lip curls just so, like the petals of a bluish rose, until they meet in a tight cluster right . . . here?" With that, he rubbed my clitoris in a feathery, semicircular motion with one finger, while using the other, nail down, to trace a thin jagged line from my navel to my slit, which became a reddish inkless tattoo for a few seconds against my growing-ever-paler skin. "See how you'd look if you were a rose? 'Rose is a rose is a rose is a rose?' " he asked, indicating the carmine "stem" he'd drawn upon my flesh.

I'd had to arc my neck at a slightly painful angle (mainly it made those tiny incisions there hurt) to see his handiwork, and even then all I had the power to do was moan a soft assent before the full force of the orgasm swept me away into a crimson, eyelids-closed private world . . .

One slightly deeper whiff of this woman's scent told me that Boyfriend couldn't be my old sanguinary sweetheart—all vampires have a special, very undefinable sweetness, like old chocolate, in their blood—but I felt a certain kinship to him anyhow . . . even though he would soon be my rival.

Poor man . . . I can understand why you want to see all of her, touch and taste and caress it all . . . even if you're willing to forgo the ripple of hair under your hands, or the moistening mat of curls surrounding that soon-to-be-plucked rose . . .

A little too much time had gone by while I was bathing in the sweet come-like stickiness of my memories; the girl's face became slightly anxious, and she asked timidly, "I know it *does* sound silly . . . I mean about the rose—but could you do it?"

Not letting the sigh I felt escape my lips (although I couldn't resist the urge to lick them), I replied, "Of course. Would you mind slipping out of your shorts and panties? It'll just take me a couple of minutes to get ready."

While the young woman slowly unzipped her shorts, her face wearing the expression of a thirteen-year-old reluctantly disrobing for the first time in gym class, I prepared the small rolling table with the clippers, five-pack of razors, shaving foam, and scissors. Then, as she wiggled out of the shorts to expose her pale green, lace-trimmed cotton briefs (I could make out the plastered-down arabesques of russet curls over her mons), I placed the long fresh towel over the seat of the barber's chair in readiness for her. As she watched me pat the white towel down on the leather seat she gulped, but stuck her thumbs down into the lacy waistband and—with her heart pounding so hard it made her left breast quiver infinitesimally—pulled down her panties, then gracefully stepped out of them. With a schoolgirl-like neatness, she bent down, knees together, and picked up the briefs and shorts, and placed them on the stool where I usually sit between customers.

You must really care about your boyfriend to put yourself through this. . . . I only wonder if he'll be so grateful once I get through with her, I asked myself as she sat down primly on the barber's chair, legs tight together, and arms gingerly placed on the padded armrests. Barely able to suppress a smile, I picked up a drape, put it around her neck (the sensation of her hair sliding over the tops of my hands as I secured the Velcro tab behind her long, thin neck was like silk rubbing against my most sensitive parts), then said, "You'll have to open up. . . . I can't do a full job otherwise."

For a second she just sat there, looking at her draped body and exposed, tousled head for a moment in the numerous mirrors surrounding the chair, a shocked expression on her face . . . until she caught on, and obediently parted her legs, so that the drape tented over them above her spread thighs. The funny part was that she had the drape hanging over her snatch. . . .

Before I picked up the clippers, I gently gathered the hem of the drape in my hand and pulled it upward, until the extra fabric was bunched in her lap. Across the room, she was reflected in all of her waving, curling, sunset-varied hues, with the deep pink rosebud center of her right in her line of vision; from the sharp intake of breath she took, I realized that she'd never seen herself so open . . . or so vulnerable.

"It won't . . . y'know, pull, when you cut it . . . will it? Going against the grain—"

"You'll be surprised how good it can feel," I assured her, before asking the standard question at the Heads-or-Tails salon. "Which do you want done first, heads or—"

"Uhm . . . I never thought about . . . Maybe my bottom . . . no, wait, better do the head," she finished reluctantly; most women go that route, even though it seems illogical. I suppose it has to do with the thought of someone touching the private parts . . . especially when no woman has done so in such intimate circumstances before.

And like most first-timers, she kept her eyes closed once I switched on the clippers. Usually, shearing takes about ten or fifteen minutes, if you're careful, and feel for any unexpected bumps or irregularities on the skull. But doing this one, this taker, took a full twenty minutes. With each slow, cautious movement of the clippers, another drift of sun-kissed hair filtered down, caressing my shins before it rested on the floor at my feet. The reddish stubble still caught the light well; from certain angles it resembled the nap on velvet, with a pearl-like white base.

And this close to her scalp, her bare neck, the odor of fresh spicy cinnamon was overpowering, achingly intense . . . but I knew I'd have to wait for my chance to savor her. Clippers seldom cause nicks serious enough for a stinging kiss. . . .

Once the last of that rippling, gorgeous hair was liberated from her scalp, I tilted the chair backward, so that her head rested on the sink drain, and—after warning her what I was going to do—ran warm water over her scalp, prior to lathering her up. By now she was beginning to relax; a thin smile even played on her lips. But she still wouldn't open her eyes, not until I'd massaged her wet scalp for a few seconds, and she fluttered her eyes open before asking, "Is the cream heated? My boyfriend, he does that before he shaves—"

"Naturally." By now, I was shaking so much inside I was afraid I might cut her for real, but once I picked up the can of heated cream and sprayed a dollop of it onto my left palm before smoothing it onto her scalp in a thin layer (too much lather and you can't see the grain of the hair—and shaving against it can be painful—but too little, and the razor pulls), my pre-vampire days hairstylists' autopilot took over. Once she'd been fully lathered, the foam barely covering the velvety bristles of her remaining hair, I washed off my hands, then pulled on the fresh pair of rubber gloves necessary before I could pick up one of the new razors from my little table. Even before I'd gone permanently nocturnal, I'd been the smoothest shaver at the salon; the trick is applying just the barest amount of pressure against the gently rounded surface.

And this time, when she closed her eyes, it was purely in ecstasy; the heightened rhythm of her breathing was unmistakable, even under the clinging drape. Whether or not a female customer I was shaving was an intended meal or not, I loved to see that blissful look on their eyes-closed faces as the gently bending steel caressed and cleaned their scalps; I suppose it's the look men strive for on the faces of women they're fucking— that away-from-it-all gratified expression.

I was so taken with stealing glances at her face in the surrounding mirrors as I worked, in fact, that her head was smooth and pearl-like before I'd had a chance to inflict a deliberate, although albeit minor dripping wound. Her eyes were still closed, so I debated whether or not to run the razor across her delicately veined white flesh once again, as if seeking stray hairs, but it would've spoiled the moment, somehow. It was my fault I'd missed my first chance at her; going back to correct my omission would be too cruel—

She's just a taker, not anything that special to you, I sternly reminded myself as I lowered the chair for a second time, to wash off the last bits of cream from her head, prior to lathering it up with an aloe-based shampoo. That she'd moan when I worked the foamy lather around her smooth, moist skin was a given . . . but what wasn't so much of a given was the way that low, purring moan made me reflexively arch my pelvis, the muscles in my inner thighs twitching in time to her barely voiced cries.

That was when I realized that her heretofore un-
named boyfriend was definitely going to get more than
he'd bargained for when he sent her here. After all,
roses and pearls are equally beautiful to more than one
beholder. . . .

Once I'd toweled her off, and then slathered a fine
coating of the most delicately scented oil I could find on
my counter onto her shorn pate (I didn't want to risk
obscuring that heady cinnamon bouquet which all but
radiated from her newly bare skin, like shimmers of
heat coming off a smooth road in the summer sun), she
timidly reached up to run a smooth hand over her
satin-fine skin . . . then gave me an unexpectedly
wicked grin, her eyes twinkling.

"I didn't think it'd feel like this," she whispered
throatily, her breasts rising and sinking deliciously beneath the drape. "I'm glad I left the best for last. . . ."

That a customer got into the whole bareness thing
wasn't unusual, but the transformation from schoolgirl
shy and demure to completely relaxed and ready for
more in this particular customer-cum-taker was enough
to make my heart lop so crazily I was afraid that it
would stop from the extraordinary effort. It was only
then that I glanced down at her waiting quim; the image of roses after the rain, when the sunlight (a still
poignant, missed memory for me) hits the petals, revealing the subtle blend of colors on each petal came to
mind . . . and this time, the scent of that brown, pow-
dery spice, mixed with her own rose oils, was all but in-
toxicating. I had to steel myself against simply going
down on her then and there, and tearing into that delicate wrinkled flesh with incisors bared openly.

Now my problem would be restraining myself; it would never do to drink too deeply, especially from such a nest of tender folds and hidden creases, lest her boyfriend (*and my enemy*, I decided) notice my handiwork too quickly before she left him.

That she would eventually leave him would now be a given; for a brief moment I wondered if *my* vampire master, he of the no-name nightspot so many years ago, had known that I'd end up leaving my previous boyfriend, as he looked and spelled and wanted me so very deeply, with a yearning beyond reason, even beyond basic desire. (Once, he'd told me that my "scent of dark coffee" was like a syrup cascading down his throat. . . .)

But still, he'd been so intuitive to her potential shorn beauty, and so eager to witness that naked splendor, that this act of taking would haunt me . . . even as it fulfilled me in a way no palm-pumping mere *man* could fully understand.

Putting on my best, most professional face (at least for the moment), I switched on the smaller set of clippers and let my hand be guided by the individual mounds and deep valleys of her flesh; once I asked her to spread her legs out wider (I'd already lowered her chair to a reclining position, the better to see her curl-hidden petals), but apart from that, neither of us spoke—or had need to. Clipping the mound of Venus is trickier than clipping the scalp; the area is tighter, and more springy under the clippers, but this time around, gathering up my concentration was an almost super non-human effort.

Freed of the damp ringlets and tufts of russet hair, her mound was a mottled pink-white (from the pressure of my fingers as I spread the flesh to accommodate the clippers), but when I applied a small disposable makeup sponge (sea sponge; it has a rougher, more French-tickler-like texture) dripping with warm water to her stubbled flesh, it soon turned an even, conch-shell pink. I couldn't resist pulling aside her inner labia, to expose the glistening slick skin within to the light, and was rewarded with a subtle upward thrust of her pelvis. That she was enjoying this gratified me, almost as much as taking a sip of her blood . . . *almost.*

The lathering was dream-like in its slowness; up, down, and around the tender, sweet-scented flesh (by now, her own unique scent formed a heady counter-point to her blood-bouquet), until the patch of foamy white was fully covered up to the tips of the stubble. Taking up the first of two fresh razors (sharpness is essential . . . and not just for my own vampiric purposes), I freed her flesh from the coating of foam stubble and drying foam, until she was almost entirely naked, more naked than she'd been at birth, in all likelihood . . . save for a last tuft of hair I'd left untouched, close to the gently rounded spot where the tip of the mount meets the tuck of the flesh hiding her clitoris.

True, that tight curve was the most difficult place to shave, but that wasn't why I left it for last. Unless I became as animal-like as the bat most non-vampires erroneously think we can turn into at will, I'd have to be cautious now . . . lest my actions become too obvious, too potentially frightening. . . .

"Could you be very still now? This is the trickiest part. . . . otherwise I might nick you." Getting the words out without bending down and biting and sucking and drinking her in was difficult, but she didn't seem to notice that anything was out of the ordinary.

As she spread herself even wider (could she be into gymnastics? I wondered), so that the last daub of nearly dried foam covering that dime-sized patch of remaining hair was almost perfectly level before me, I had to release some of the pent-up desire in me . . . if not my thirsting desire, then my sexual wanting.

Using both hands, I gently fanned my fingers over her taut lower belly, her tight thighs, not letting myself touch her exposed petal-softness, her intricate folds and crevices of glistening flesh, until I was sure that my hands wouldn't shake too much. I only needed a tiny nick, not a bloodbath . . . even though I would have loved to have felt her cinnamon warmth coursing over me in hot, spurting runnels. . . .

Taking up the second of two razors I'd used on her, I let the sharp steel bite ever so superficially into her pale skin on the downstroke. I don't even think she felt the nick, it was so slight, but my mouth flooded with burning saliva when I saw the tiny dark pearl of blood rise up in all its spicy-warm splendor.

"Uh, oh, I drew a bit of . . . lemme get the pencil," I mumbled, before grabbing the styptic wand off the little table . . . and then clutching it so tightly in my fingers that it bent out of shape as I knelt down and ran my tongue over the welling beads of ruby sustenance, before my incisors bore down on the pliant, perfumed flesh of her outer labia, her mons, her inner thigh. . . .

For a moment, a deeply shamed, yet animalistically exalted moment, I felt a stab of fear-pleasure—here I was, being so obvious, so greedy, and with an uninitiated taker. But in the next moment, as I stopped my inhalation-like feeding, I realized that she was moving her pelvis and hips in time with my movements, my feasting on her very inner essence.

Sated enough to stop what I was doing, I guiltily wiped my bloody lips clean with the back of one hand (then licked said hand with a fly-flick of my tongue), before standing up between her still-splayed out legs, and letting my gaze meet her own. Reaching down with her right hand, she gently touched the place where I'd been sucking out her blood, gave me a smile, one that did reach up to those memory-of-sunlit-leaves green eyes of hers, and then said softly, "I suppose I can tell my boyfriend that even my rose had some thorns . . ." before beckoning me back to sup once more on her glistening feast between her outspread legs.

But the best part of what she said was the way she made "boyfriend" sound so casual, like something ultimately fungible after all. . . .

Later, without needing to ask, she simply agreed to come to the salon on a thrice-weekly schedule, for "more of what you did tonight." I didn't ask her name; eventually, she became Rose for me, and that was all either of us needed. But that first night, as she dressed and covered her pearlescent scalp with a scarf she'd brought along in her shorts pocket, I busied myself with a little gift—a token of future losses, actually—for her soon-to-be-ex-boyfriend.

It's funny, but if you take those pink-and-red colored specialty condoms (like I said, the Heads-or-Tails offered occasional "extras") and—after opening the packages—twist and bunch them just so, then attach them with plastic-covered twist ties (green ones, naturally—we keep them on hand for securing garbage bags full of clippings) to those wooden sticks we use to stir hair dye, they'll look an awful lot like rosebuds.

Maybe her boyfriend did find my gesture touching (Rose never felt the need to say, later), but from my point of view—not knowing just how faithful he might be—I was only protecting my investment against blood that stank of moldy grapes and bread long gone stale.

THE WAGER

Anna Nymus

A STRANGER IN a roomful of strangers. What makes this one special? I nudge Odette. We are standing near the jukebox in a corner of the bar. "You see that guy next to the wall?" She looks over. "Him?" she says dismissively. Probably doesn't see what I see. Pale, angular face, well-cut dark hair falling over his forehead. Not drinking much, looks down into his beer as if, for all he cares, he were alone in this place. The gesture he makes, lifting his head to flick the hair back out of his eyes. It is because of this I know I can take him.

Odette glances back at me. She knows what I'm up to.

"Listen," I say. "This guy's a Scorpio."

"Scorpio, is he?"

I nudge her again. "I'm telling you. He's a Scorpio. Aren't you going to ask me how I know?"

"You met him at astrology class," she drawls, with that indolent sarcasm for which she is famous.

"Never set eyes on him before in my life."

"I get it. He's a Scorpio because . . . of the way he drinks beer?"

I put her hand against my cheek. Her hand is ice because I'm burning. "If there's one of them, just one, in a whole room full of strangers, I know."

She lights a cigarette, tips back her head to let the smoke out, very slowly, through her nostrils. "Yeah," she says. "So he's a Scorpio." She unzips her jacket, takes out the onyx charm I gave her in place of a wedding ring, tosses it in the air. Now she's got that smile I've been expecting. I have to win it back, to win her all over again, to keep love going.

He's sitting in the corner, leaning on his elbow. Saturday night, the place is crowded. Hair oil, perfume, loud music, bitter smoke, and he sits there staring at a glass of beer. I have to squeeze past the man standing next to him. I push in sideways, rest my elbow against the bar. So now I'm here, I'm looking down at him.

In a few minutes he's aware of me. He'll look up, won't be interested, not much, in what he sees. Dark circles around dark eyes. Nevertheless I'll take him.

He reaches out for the pack of cigarettes on the bar. I reach faster. I shake the pack, hold one out to him. He frowns up at me, doesn't smile, holds my eyes for a few seconds, shrugs, takes a cigarette. We repeat the same little game with his lighter. Again he gives in. Moving closer now I light his cigarette. I wonder what he makes of me, smiling down at him the way a conqueror, sure of conquest, smiles.

"Seen you here before?" he says. Good sign, his having to speak first. Me, I keep silent. I move closer, getting my thigh up close against his thigh. He clears his throat, shifts about on the bar stool.

I say nothing, more tension. My thigh hard against his hard thigh. His fingers play with the lighter. My fingers move over his hand, taking it from him. This time, when he looks up at me, he doesn't look away.

"I told my lover you were a Scorpio," I say, and fall silent again.

He has light eyes, a rim of darkness around the pupil. He's younger than I thought, more vulnerable. He passes his tongue across his lips. Looking up at me, looking away, his eyes drawn back to mine, he says, "How'd you know that?"

"Can't you guess?"

By now he's wondering if he should get up fast, leave his cigarettes, get the hell out of here. He glances at the man next to me. Male proximity. It won't do him any good. The place is too crowded. If he takes off, he's going to look like a man in flight. He flicks his ash with the edge of his thumb, puts his cigarette between his lips, straightens his shoulders.

I take a drink from his glass without saying a word, so now he laughs, in spite of himself. A good laugh, boyish, yielding. There's a fine line of sweat on his upper lip. He's watching me as if I were a snake charmer.

Maybe I am.

Imperceptibly, he leans toward me, closing the tension, locking it between us.

I will put my left hand on his shoulder. It takes a special courage to do this. That's what Odette admires. When I reach out to touch him there will be no turning back.

I have placed myself fully between him and the man next to me. I glance down at his lap. There's that distance, impossible between strangers, between the place I'm touching now and where I'm going. I give him time to figure it out, to refuse me. My hand grows heavy on his shoulder. I take the cigarette from his lips, set it burning into the glass ashtray. I keep looking at him. A few years ago, on a good night, when I was new to it, this was enough, sometimes. My hand moves to his waist, comes to rest on the leather belt, takes hold of the thick buckle, plays with it lightly.

We are so damned close to one another, my breast pushed hard against his shoulder, my knee moving to push his knee against the bar, I can't tell for sure who is breathing. I guess that's my breath in the dark hair that curls over his ears.

My hand moves slowly, willing him to stop me if he still can, over the rough cloth pants, his body hammering against my palm. I stroke along his bulge, around it, pretending this isn't serious. It's up to him. My touch is delicate, he can ignore it if he wants to. Fingertips and nails, I stroke, I size him up, I trace his shape. Then I cusp him with my whole hand as though ready to take him. But I don't. He draws his breath in with anticipation. I hover, cusp him. Demand that he give himself over to me. I know what will happen. I send Odette a glance saying, You're gonna lose that bet, honey, right now. He's getting there. He'll let me know he's mine.

He can't wait to let me know. He is sweating. He pushes against me desperate to feel my enclosure, to bulge even larger, to grow out of himself, out of his mind, to be gripped.

I'm not moving, my hand is absolutely not moving in

his lap. He's the one who has to move so there can be no doubt which of us wants this encounter between strangers, which of us asks for it. I keep my eyes on Odette while he lifts himself on his bar stool to press himself again, then again into my hand.

"*Plaisir d'amour, ne dure qu'un moment . . .*" Odette, sending me a message from the jukebox. We are rocking here in a dark corner of the bar, his sex filling my hand. I have unzipped him. I curl my fingers around him, stroking. "Don't come, make it last, don't come," I whisper into his ear, knowing Odette has started counting.

He's trying to keep his breath steady, face calm, shoulders still, hands gripping the bar. He's biting his lip hard. I keep stroking. Across the room the song has started up again. Odette, promising what comes later.

Before he comes, his eyes glazed with the effort to pretend nothing is happening, I glance over at Odette. She is sipping her drink as she leans against the jukebox, watching.

I hold up the onyx charm, flipping it between my fingers. That's when his body starts to shake. He jerks back from me once, his boot sliding against my calf, his left hand grabbing at the ashtray.

On a scale from one to ten, I would say that was an eight plus orgasm. I'd like to hang around to see him recover. But Odette wouldn't like it if I lingered.

from THE FERMATA

Nicholson Baker

TOWARD THE MIDDLE of September, Marian's sexual
interest inexplicably abated. She put all her dildi and
appliances in the drawer that had once held David's
sweaters. The last two toys she had ordered—a tiny
vibe, teasingly canine in appearance but molded from
an impeccably *comme il faut* piece of pickled okra, and a
giant Armande Klockhammer Signature Model—she
didn't even bother to try out before putting them in
storage. She felt a mild snobbish contempt for people
who devoted so much of their free time to solo sex-play.
Her perennial garden, for example, was far more satis-
fying than a bunch of pastless, futureless orgasms. She
read bulb catalogs avidly. After much study she ordered
several hundred tulip bulbs from Mack's. When they arrived, via UPS, she gently deflected the eagerly scrotal
leer of her friend John in the brown truck. It felt excit-

ing and strange to be more than a sexual being, to have interests. As she looked over the boxes of bulbs, however, she realized that she would need help cutting the beds and planting them all, so she hired the neighbor kid, Kevin.

Ever since she had been mowing her own lawn, she had lost touch with young Kevin. He seemed to have grown an inch or two. He had gone out for the high jump, and he had acquired a girlfriend named Sylvie, who he said was "a really special person." For a whole weekend and three cool late afternoons he and Marian worked together preparing the soil in the beds with bags of peat and then setting in the bulbs. The dirt was cool through Marian's gloves. After shyly asking whether she would mind, Kevin brought over his radio. At first she was a little irritated by the sound, which disturbed her bucolic alpha-state—but over time several of the songs separated themselves from the others. In one, a woman sang something about Solitude standing in the doorway. She sang, "Her palm is split with a flower with a flame." Marian kept time to this song, first with her troweling, and then with her chin. When she had heard it the second time, she asked Kevin (feeling a little shy herself), "Who does this song?"

Kevin looked up. "Suzanne Vega."

"Ah," said Marian. "I like it."

"Yeah, it's pretty good," said Kevin. He was impossible to read. He dropped another dark bulb in a hole and gently mounded soil around it. Marian glanced at him several times. He had a gray track-and-field T-shirt over a gray sweatshirt. When he pushed on the earth over one of her bulbs, she imagined the muscle in the side of his arm, as she had seen it when he had had his shirt off that day, long ago, at the beginning of summer, before she had learned to mow. And later, when the song came on again, he looked up at her and smiled and then went back to planting—and Marian noticed that his ears were quite red.

She watered the bulbs in and forgot about them. The ground began to look cold—three long beds of very cold bulbs. As winter hit, Marian became caught up in a battle with a developer who wanted to build another mall outside of town. It was going to be enormous and in its own way wonderful—but there was already a shopping center with a discount chain in it that was working under chapter eleven, and the downtown would suffer, as it always did. She went out on several dates with a man she met at the mall meetings, and while she enjoyed talking to him (he was one of those men who have a passionate interest in some particular writer which at first seems sincere, and then finally ends up seeming almost arbitrary—in his case it was Rilke: he seemed to be getting things from Rilke that he could have gotten from any number of poets, while missing whatever it was that Rilke had uniquely), she nonetheless didn't want to do anything more than kiss him cordially in her driveway.

When spring finally came, she went out every day to her tulip beds to watch for activity. It was an unusually dry hot spring, and she felt that she should water to give her beds a good start, but she despaired at her hose. The faucet still leaked tiresomely. The sprayer was rusty. What would make her bulbs really happy, it suddenly occurred to her, was if she could get a plumber to adapt her own Pollenex showerhead so that it would fit on the end of the hose. She needed a very light, very delicate but insistent spray for her tulips—no garden sprayer could offer that. She also thought that the hose water was much too cold—she felt that the bulbs would do better with warmer water. She realized that she wasn't thinking all that rationally, but her idea nonetheless was: hook up the garden hose to the shower-pipe, run the hose out the bathroom window, and fix the Pollenex showerhead onto the terminal end. Other ideas of interest followed on this one; she called a plumber.

The plumber was a thin derisive man with the usual plumber body-smell who rolled his eyes at her plan, told her she could have done it herself, but agreed, since he was there, to do it for her. He fitted the hose ends and the Pollenex with Gardena quick-clamp adapters so that they could be quickly reconfigured for interior showering or exterior gardening applications. The shower pipe looked exotic when he was done, knobbed with hex nuts and adapters, but the system when tested worked quite well. And the plumber, as he cleaned up, was cheerful, pleased by now that he had built something he had never built before, and that he would be able to tell his partner about the nutty job this lady had gotten him to do. He even showed her how to use Teflon tape and was expansive about its merits over older kinds of sealant. He carried his heavy red toolbox out to his truck and drove away.

Over the next few days Marian took her early-morning shower and then opened the window, hooked up the shower-hose arrangement, and turned on the taps to water her tulips. She used only the fine pulse-mist settings, treating her plants as she would want to be treated herself. The tulips responded with enthusiasm—after a week her beds were popping with color.

They knew the difference between water from a shower, meant for human use, and water from a crude leaky outdoor faucet. She sat on an aluminum chair with the sun on her legs, reading *The Machine in the Garden*. Every so often she glanced up at her tulips. She felt happy. She had planned this to happen and it had happened: she had delayed gratification and now she was getting the payoff. Young Kevin should see what they had done together, she thought, but when she called, Kevin's sour mother told her that he was at practice. Just as well, just as well, she thought. She began to give some consideration to her drawerful of dildae. But she didn't need any of that; no, she'd moved beyond that.

Just then Kevin's little gray cat with white paws showed up on her lawn, making untoward noises and acting oddly. Quite recently it, she, had been a kitten. Now she was clearly in heat, probably for the first time—and very irresponsible it was of Kevin or Kevin's mother not to have had her fixed! She crawled along with her forepaws very low on the ground, making low desperate mezzo-mewings, her tail jerking back, her little narrow feline hips flaunting and twitching in the air, her rear paws working with quick tiptoe steps. Marian could see her gray-furred opening; wetness gleamed from within. She went over and pressed her finger lightly against the cat's tiny slit; gratefully, the cat returned the pressure and tiptoed ardently in place. This was a cat in the grip of a new idea. Wiping her finger on the grass, Marian found that she had gotten hot looking at this creature's fluttery haunchings. There was a purity and seriousness to the cat's simple wish to be fucked immediately that Marian found refreshing. The cat didn't want love—it wanted cat-cock.

Marian was not a committed zoophile, though—at least she didn't think of herself as one. True, she and her best friend in sixth grade had made her friend's black Labrador shoot two quick clear squirts of come once by gently squeezing his dense buried bulb as he lay on his back with his legs open and his eyes half closed, but one swallow doesn't make a summer. Marian was a fan of human cock, for better or worse. (Dogdick did still have a certain appeal to her, in part because when it emerged it had a clitoral, almost hermaphroditic quality: something bisexual in her was triggered by the sight of it.) Mentally she again reviewed her dildos—how could she have (one or two late nights excepted) snubbed them all winter? The idea of running herself a bath, and then straddling the cold edge of the tub so that all her weight was on the soft place between her vadge and her ass, began to seem attractive. She could take one of the middle-sized dildi and swish it around in the bathwater and shake it off, so that it waggled obscenely, and stick it down on the edge of the tub and squirt Astroglide all over it. She could arrange herself over it, supporting herself with her hands on the edge of the tub, looking down past her hanging breasts at the slick dildo as it slowly disappeared into her sex-hair and found its thick way up inside her. She went inside to do just this, but by the time she had actually drawn the bath and gotten into it, she was much too aroused to do tame things in her bathroom. She got out and dried off and slipped on a dress. She had a new plan. She wanted to have a full-fledged Betty Dodsonian PC-muscled clasm outside in honor of her tulip garden.

She went out in her bare feet, scouting a location. Kevin's cat had disappeared. After some pacing and gazing, she picked a place between two of the tulip beds, near where she had seen Kevin's ears get red when they had talked about the "Solitude stands in the doorway" song. The problem was, what could she use as a stable base to affix her dildos to? The grass blades would be a ticklish irritant. Back inside, she tried a rectangular black lacquer tray in the kitchen, but it had a raised edge that, when she put it on a chair and experimentally sat down on it, hurt her butt. She considered a Thanksgiving serving platter but didn't like the idea of its breaking; she pondered a small plastic plate left over from a premium frozen dinner, but it wasn't heavy enough. Finally she went into her dining room and took the tea service off of her grandmother's brass tray. The tea service itself was undistinguished, but the tray was a Viennese beauty, chased with circles of bouquets and thick-scaled fish and pine cones and mythical panthery creatures in high relief. In the middle was a very stylized sun—it looked like a fried egg—and this proved to be the perfect surface on which to fix a dildo's suction cup.

The famed male dancer at the Golden Banana, Armande Klockhammer, Jr., had only once in his distinguished career consented to have a lost-wax mold made of the trilogy-in-flesh that had opened so many doors for him. Along the underside of the slightly upcurved and alarmingly lifelike high-grade silicone cock-stalk, Armande's own signature, taken directly from the licensing contract, ran, in such a way that the two bas-relief *m*'s of his surname appeared right over what would have been, had this been his actual dick, its most sensitive part. Marian arranged her virgin Armande Klockhammer Signature Model, along with many of its veteran colleagues, on a linen napkin unfolded on her brass tray and bore them out into the garden. She put the tray down in the thick grass in the chosen spot, leaving room on either side for her to plant her feet. There was a slight haze in the sky, so that it was sunny, but not uncomfortably so. When she moved the napkin aside, the light glinted on the tray's ancient pattern, and, once she had squirted copious Astroglide over its head, on the surface of her chosen dildo as well—which looked opulently nasty poking up from that heirloom.

Then, playing hard-to-get now that she knew she had Armande where she wanted him, she went for a blithe little walk. She was wearing a jumper printed with big loose flowers and nothing underneath. She went to her mailbox, checked that the mail had been delivered, but left it in there. She nodded to a bicyclist going by—he was wearing a kind of skin-tight black cycling shorts that she normally didn't like, but now she didn't mind seeing his thigh definition. She stood at the end of her driveway for several minutes with her arms crossed, breathing deep breaths of spring air and feeling peaceful and content, or playing at looking like the woman out in the garden breathing deeply and feeling content, while actually part of her was thinking over what dildic wickedness was waiting for her in her backyard. On her way back, she bent and felt a leaf of one of the peonies in the tractor tire in her front yard, very casually, giving the road the chance to appreciate her shape under her dress, and murmured to herself, "Hmm, I think it may be time to do some watering." She went in and got the water temperature just right in her shower, and then drew the hose into the bathroom window and hooked it to the shower spigot. Outside, she turned the stopcock on (the plumber had fixed it so that she could turn the flow of water on and off at the end of the hose) and toured her side yard, sending a frolicsome misty spray from her mobile water-source over the grass and over the mock orange leaves. She hummed "Private Dancer." She heard a truck drive past on the road.

When she rounded the back of the house, she surprised a deer who had wandered by, drawn by the tasty-looking tulip blossoms. It appeared to be licking the pink head of the Armande Klockhammer with its equally pink tongue. "Now, now, enough of that!" Marian called, and the deer sprang away. She glanced around to verify that she was indeed in private, and put her foot up on her lawn chair and hiked up her jumper, holding it in a one-handed bunch just below her breasts, and directed the crown of water-jets on her clit-site. The water was just right. "Oh, nice," she said, watching the flow disappear into the grass. The idea that she could carry her daily shower around with her, outside, pleased her quite a lot. She dropped her dress and began watering again, working up the nodding tulip beds. Her maraschino tingled. She pretended to notice for the first time something alien and fleshy sticking up, pinkly out of place in the general verdancy beyond the near bed of tulips. "What's this now?" She pointed the shower-water at it (making sure to rinse away any deer saliva). "What's this sex organ doing sticking straight up in my garden? Does it need something to fuck?" She pulled up her dress. "Is this what Armande wants?" Again she pointed the showerhead up between her legs, now turning it to PULSE. Big dick-shaped bullets of water thumped against the skin surrounding her clit-pearl, against her vadge, and, as she rocked her hips, tickled against the poor-relation sensitivities of her asshole. "Oh man," she said, loving it. "Listen you, if you liked that Bambi-tongue, you're going to *love* my hot little box." The dildo was unresponsive. She walked closer, confronting it. "Oh? So you're not sure? You're not even sure you want to be in my hot little *ass?* You're shy? Well, I'm sorry, you have no choice now—you're going to have to fuck me in the ass." She took the bottle of Astroglide from her jumper-pocket and slid it between her cheeks and squirted herself with it until it trickled down her leg. Then she put her feet on either side of the brass tray and slowly squatted down until she felt the Klockhammer brushing against her butt-muscle. She directed the showerhead back on her clit. She didn't care if her dress got soaked or not. Her thighs began to tremble with the effort of supporting herself over the dildismic pressure without sliding down on it. Finally she couldn't help herself, and she opened her asshole to its big head and sat all the way down on it, until her cheek touched the cold ornate metal of the tray. She rocked on the feeling of a hefty dickful of pleasure up her ass, adjusting to it. Her drenched dress hung over her thighs. She was fucking Armande Klockhammer's autograph! God, it felt good.

"Hello?" came a voice. Marian looked up to see young Kevin and a girl standing hand in hand a little way off. She supposed the girl was Sylvie, Kevin's new girlfriend. Kevin was looking recently showered, spruced up, and proud of himself, though momentarily

puzzled. Marian saw his eyes skip down over her exposed, wet legs. The two of them were wearing matching red-and-white-striped polo shirts. Marian made a
quick attempt to pull her dress down and over some of
the sex toys next to her. She began watering the tulips
with little flips of the showerhead, as if she were con-
ducting a Sousa march.

"Hi," she said. "Pardon me, I was just doing a little
watering. Come over. Let me turn this off. I had a
plumber rig it up for me. Are you Sylvie?"

"Yes, hi," said Sylvie. Sylvie leaned and shook Marian's hand. She was a petite, perky, small-breasted girl
with long light-brown hair and a pleasant sly sharp-
nosed face. Marian liked her immediately.

Kevin said, "My mom told me you called, so we
thought we'd come over and say hello."

"I just wanted you to see all these tulips," said Marian. "They turned out well, I think. Thank you for help-
ing me with them."

Kevin nodded. "I like the crinkly ones." He turned to
Sylvie. "Last fall I helped her plant all these."

"They're really really pretty," Sylvie agreed. There
was an awkward silence. From a distant part of the yard
there came an odd hissing sound. Kevin's gray cat appeared from behind one of the mock oranges. A huge
golden chewn-eared stray was on top of her. Kevin's cat
crept forward a few inches and then stopped, and the
gold cat, holding Kevin's cat down and biting her neck
quite hard, made tiny jerks of its hindquarters, holding
its tail low and fluffed. The two animals, who didn't
seem to like each other much, stared at nothing at all
while they fucked.

"Oh jeepers," said Kevin.

"You really should have taken her to the vet, Kevin," said Marian, though she said it gently.

"I was planning to."

"I can take a kitten if there are some," said Sylvie brightly, thinking ahead. "Maybe even two."

Marian smiled at her. "That's solved, then. Well!" It was time for them to be off. "I'm really glad you two dropped by. It's very nice to meet you, Sylvie."

"Nice to meet you. But can I ask you something?" said Sylvie. "What are all those?" She pointed to the sex toys laid out on the white linen napkin. Marian's dress didn't really hide them effectively.

"I don't know that we should get into that," said Marian.

"Okay, sorry," said Sylvie. "I kind of know what they are anyway—I mean, it's obvious, but I just want to know what you're doing with them out here. Are you planning on burying them or planting them or something?"

Kevin's ears were changing color. He was readjusting his notion of his employer. Sylvie just looked friendly and sly and curious.

Marian said, "No, I'm not burying them. I just thought it would be exciting to try out a few of them outdoors, and I wasn't sure which ones I would want. It seemed like such a nice setting, my own backyard, with the new parrot tulips."

"Can I look at one?" said Sylvie.

Marian passed her the most decorous dildo—a medium-sized clear lucite thick-veined figurine that the catalog called the Ice Princess. Sylvie handled it carefully, using her fingertips, not, it seemed, out of repugnance, but out of politeness for another's treasures.

"Sylvie," said Kevin in an undertone. "I think she probably wants us to go."

"She's welcome to take a look if she wants," said Marian casually. The Klockhammer deep in her ane was now beginning to reassert itself; it was silencing any objections she might otherwise have had to showing two teenagers wearing matching striped shirts her fuckable toys.

"Can I see that really long one, with the two ends?" said Sylvie.

"Ah yes—this is my Royal Welsh Fusilier. Here."

"Wowsers!" Sylvie held the two dick-ends together, jerking on them so that the movable foreskins wrinkled and stretched in tandem. She offered one end to Kevin, who inspected it with fascination in spite of himself.

"I don't exactly get why you would need something this long with two ends," he said.

Marian hesitated. "Any number of reasons."

"One of which is," said Sylvie to Kevin, "if you misbehave with Karen in any way ever again, I'll put one end right up your fanny and make you jump in your next meet with it in."

"Karen is over," said Kevin. Deferentially he thanked Marian, handing his end directly back to her. "Where did you purchase all these things?" he asked, with an air of serious inquiry.

"Oh, from a place in San Francisco," said Marian. She was using every ounce of willpower she had to keep from announcing to the two of them that she had a massive dildungsroman installed in her butt.

"Maybe sometime you could give us the address," said Kevin, still very serious, very grown up. "We might want to order something or other. Right, Syl?"

"You never know," said Sylvie.

Marian looked at them both and laughed happily. "God it's nice to see young love," she said. "Are you two lovers, then?"

They both nodded. "We've made love thirty-two times in two months," said Sylvie proudly. "In fact," she continued, putting a fond arm around Kevin's waist, "we were just going out for a little 'drive,' because Kevin's mother doesn't like us going up to his room anymore—which I can understand."

"Ah, a little 'drive,' " said Marian. She looked at Kevin with amused surprise—the employer surprised at the precocity of the employee.

"Yeah," Kevin agreed, gesturing vaguely in the direction of the road. "We'll probably go on over to the fish hatchery."

"Well, terrific," Marian said. "Have a glorious glorious time, you two. I wish I could . . . I mean, I wish you well." She shifted a little on the brass tray and felt the thick steadfast dilderstatesman issuing official pleasure-briefings down her legs and up to the warm unforgotten Fijis of her nipples. It was so fucking *hard*—so hard to keep from saying the things she wanted to say with it deep in there: she wanted to yank up her wet dress for them and say, "Go on and fuck each other silly! Take a good look at this monster cock jammed up my butt! I want you to look right at my asshole crammed with this big fat *dick* and then go out and fuck and suck each other and slam your bodies together!" Her skin prickled with the almost irresistible wish to be obscene. But all she said was, "I must say, I envy you both a little. I'm just sorry I can't get up and see you off . . ."

Sylvie was immediately full of concern. She touched Marian lightly on the arm. "Are you okay? Can we help you up? You know your dress has gotten a little wet."

"I know, I know," said Marian, "I've been watering everywhere."

"Everywhere?" said Sylvie. "Isn't it kind of cold?"

"The water's warm. It's from my shower. Feel." Marian turned the stopcock on and whisked the shower-head spray once over Sylvie's outstretched hand.

"Feels really nice," said Sylvie thoughtfully.

"The tulips love it," said Marian. "In fact, will you two do me a favor and pick some for each other before you go? As my present to you? Pick the ones you like most. The Etruscan Prune variety is my favorite at the moment, but choose whichever ones you want."

Sylvie and Kevin liked this idea a lot and set to work assembling reciprocal bouquets. Now that their eyes were off Marian, she was free to move on the tray again and make pleasure noises in a whispery undertone. She watched them circle her beds. She imagined them all breathless and loving and wide-eyed in a shady spot near the fish hatchery. They were beautiful—fit, healthy, incredibly young—so inexperienced that they thought that their two-digit courtship, or coitship, made them seasoned fuckers. She knew so much more than they did. She lifted the sodden hem of her dress just a little and pointed the showerhead between her legs and let it flood her twat-cleavage. "That's not nearly enough, Kevin—pluck more!" she called gaily, wanting to risk his hearing the irrepressible vulval surges and catches in her voice.

When they stood in front of her again, holding their tulip bunches out to her for her admiration, she pronounced both arrangements equally lovely and told them to give them to each other. This they did with great ceremony.

"Thank you!" said Kevin to Sylvie.

"Thank you!" said Sylvie to Kevin.

They kissed. It appeared that their mouths were a good match. Marian, who normally felt squirmy and put off when she was a witness to heavy public pair-bonding, watched this particular kiss with nothing but good feeling. She *was* the public, after all. There was some tongue-action, but it had the license of youth and looked like it felt better than it looked. They hugged each other hard; Sylvie's heel went behind Kevin's and she used the leverage to press her blue-jeaned mound into him.

When they stopped, Marian said, "What a great kiss! You two are obviously *great* kissers. You must be beautiful when you . . . make love. Your bodies fit together so well. I wish I could—" She shook her head ruefully, her hand on her heart, and let them laugh at the impossibility of what she was thinking, so that they could start to get used to the idea. Then she slapped her hands on her legs and said, "I tell you what. If you would like to borrow any of these toys, feel free. Really. I don't make any great claims for them—I'm sure you can do without them, but who knows, just for fun . . ."

They looked indecisive.

Marian exerted the slightest additional pressure. "Pick one—or a few, even." She felt a trickle of sweat on her back.

"What do you think, Kevin?" said Sylvie.

Kevin shrugged. "Sure, I guess, yeah."

Sylvie and Kevin knelt, not minding apparently that

their knees got instantly soaked in the wet grass. Sylvie's face, though averted, was very close to Marian's. "Which one would you recommend?" the girl finally asked, having touched them all lightly.

"Mmm, well—" This was just too much for Marian. She felt her resistance give way completely. "My current favorite is one I just got," she said. "It's called the Armande Klockhammer. As you may know, Armande Klockhammer, Jr., is, or was, a male stripper at the Golden Banana. It's kind of big, actually. Almost too big, depending on where you need it to go."

"Which one is it?" Sylvie asked.

Marian cleared her throat. "I'm afraid I can't show it to you right now."

"Why not?" Sylvie looked at her with innocent curiosity.

"I just can't."

"But why?" Sylvie insisted. "Where is it?"

"It's in use," said Marian. She looked at her two young friends and then down at her wet dress.

Kevin looked surprised. He had finally pieced it together. "You mean that all the time we've been here it's been . . ."

Marian took a deep breath. "Up my ass, yes."

"Up your . . . It's not in your . . . it's in your . . . ?" Sylvie, pointing to parts of herself to clarify her exclamation, looked genuinely surprised.

"It feels super, I must tell you," said Marian. "But that's not the crazy thing. The crazy thing is how badly I want to show it to you. While it's in there, I mean. I'm doing everything I can to keep from hauling this dress up right now and leaning back and showing you how good it feels stuffed up my tight butt. Oh man! Just thinking about it gets me going. Are you repulsed?"

They continued to look a little surprised, but not repulsed.

Marian went on. "I'm afraid you caught me at a particular moment. Kevin, you can attest to the fact that I don't normally talk this way."

"She doesn't at all, no," Kevin agreed.

"It's dildo talk, frankly," Marian went on. "It's the way I talk when I'm sitting on a big fat artificial dick. What can I say? My butt is stretched so damn tight right now—I wish you could see, I really do. I wish I could show you, and I wish when you saw it in my ass you'd take off all your clothes and make love for me right here. Is that so unthinkable? I don't think it's so unthinkable. Kevin, I was so good last summer. Do you realize that? I thought about your cock quite a number of times, I thought about sucking it and jerking it off—I even thought of putting a sprig of parsley in your tiny little cockhole, and yet I never once did *anything!* And now you've found Sylvie, this wonderful friendly open person, who probably sucks your cock beautifully, and it makes me feel so good that you've found her—it makes me want to *see her* suck on your cock. God, I wish I could show you what I have up my ass right now. It feels so fucking hot." She paused. "See, that's a sample of dildo talk."

Sylvie was the first to speak. "You can show it to us," she said. "We won't mind."

"Really?" said Marian. "Well, you take off all your clothes, then, both of you. I'm not going to show you anything until all your clothes are off. Take them off."

Obediently Sylvie and Kevin took off their pants and underpants and pulled off their matching striped shirts.

When the dangling and tugging and hopping had ceased and they stood naked in front of her, Marian couldn't help whistling in amazement. Their bodies were so simple and perfect. Sylvie's flattish slanting breasts, with sharp confident little suck-tips, were especially good for the soul. Kevin's white straight penis lobbed and loitered below his tight brown balls; he had a Dennis-the-Menace touch of hair around each of his nipples. Marian had to turn the Pollenex on and point it up her dress in order to recover her seducer's concentration.

"Now show us," said Sylvie challengingly, conscious that her revealed beauty gave her power. She ran her fingers over her stomach and brushed the side of her hand casually against Kevin's cock. "Show us what's up your . . ."

"Ah, you're such a beautiful couple," said Marian. "You're made to fuck each other. I'll show you when it's the right time. Right now, I need you to show me how pretty you are together. Show me how you like to suck cock, Sylvie honey. I want to see your pretty lips on that hot cockmeat. Kiss it for me."

Sylvie, compelled by the conviction in Marian's voice, knelt and kissed a path down Kevin's cock until she came to its head, and then she opened her lips and let it fill her mouth. As he watched her and moaned, Kevin's mouth mirrored Sylvie's. He was standing with his hands crossed lightly at the wrists behind his back, his hips pushed forward, looking down at his girlfriend. As he firmed up, Sylvie's jaw was forced open wider and her tongue was pushed down, and Marian was pleased to see her develop a cocksucker's temporary double chin, which, because in reality the girl had nothing approaching a double chin, only made her face look younger and more captivatingly innocent.

"That's so nice, so pretty, that pretty sucking," said Marian, letting her showerhead do the talking for her. Areas of grass near her legs were getting a marshy gleam.

Sylvie turned and looked at her. Her eyes were dreamy with confused arousal. "Please show me and Kev what you have up your fanny," she said again. She added rhetorical weight to her request by stroking three times on Kevin's cock.

Marian pulled her dress up so that it was very high on her thighs, but not so high that anything was revealed. She lifted her weight on her hands for a moment and then swiveled her hips. "It's all slicked up with lubricant. It feels so snazzy in there. I want it in there always. I want to show it to you as it fucks my butt, but I need some inspiration. I need to see your cute little asshole first, Sylvie. That's only fair. Squat right over my feet—I want to see your beautiful back and your open ass and your hot little asshole while you suck your boyfriend's cock."

"But—" said Sylvie.

"You know you want to show me everything about your body. You're not ashamed of anything, are you? You're proud of your body. You know you want me to look right at your ass while you suck that luscious dick. Don't you?"

"Yes," said Sylvie. "I want you to watch me sucking on Kevin." She planted her feet on either side of Marian's ankles and squatted, her back to the older woman. Marian twisted the showerhead to PULSE and aimed the spray in circles over Sylvie's ass globes.

"Pull your cheeks apart—I can't quite see you, and I need to see you," said Marian. Sylvie got two handfuls of her ass and pulled up, and Marian saw the dark little dot where they met and joined. She pointed the water's pulse straight at it. Sylvie arched her back to get a more direct hit; her breaths began to come harder and more irregularly through her nose. Her hair bobbed as her mouth emptied and filled with cock.

"*That's* what I like to see," said Marian. "Kevin, I wish you could see how beautiful Sylvie is when she sucks on your cock with her sexy ass all open and clean." Kevin looked up at her as she said this, and Marian, as she continued to murmur encouragement, gave him a brief secret show, looking straight at him as she jogged her tits under her dress and pinched her nipples through the fabric. Her fingers were wet, so they left dark marks where they had been. Then, when she knew she had his allegiance, she said, "Kevin, do you mind if I tickle Sylvie's pretty butt with the flowers she gave you? You want her to feel good while she sucks your big dick, don't you?"

"Go ahead," said Kevin thickly.

Marian leaned forward and brushed the tulip heads across Sylvie's shoulders and down her back. She slapped them lightly back and forth on the insides of the girl's fine thighs and up against her popped-out clit. "Ooo, she likes it," she said. Then she turned the tulips in a circle over Sylvie's asshole. "Do you like my flowers tickling your pretty butt? I bet you do."

Sylvie said something affirmative and sucked some more. Then she stopped. She didn't let go of Kevin's shiny cock, but she said, "Could I use your bathroom for a second? I'm dying."

"Sure," said Marian. "But you don't have to. Why lose time? Just let it go. I'll spray it away. Piss it right out on my feet."

"Pee on your feet?" Sylvie exclaimed. "No way! I can't do that."

"Of course you can," Marian said. "What's the harm? Just keep sucking that tasty dick and relax. When I have a big rubber dick up my asshole I like to see everything. I *want* to see it. I want to feel it spray out all over my feet—warm up these lonely toesies." She played the showerhead spray insistently over Sylvie's climb-folds. "Suck and push, honey," she urged. "It'll feel good, believe me. Arch your back so I can see."

Sylvie resumed sucking Kevin's cock.

"Push for me," said Marian. "Push that piss out." But nothing happened.

"I'm really sorry—I can't," said Sylvie. "I'm a little shy about that in front of Kev."

"Ah, I see. Kevin? You don't mind, do you? Of course not. In fact, you know what? I'd love to see a little dribble of piss come out of that big friendly cock. I bet that would help Sylvie relax." Marian moved one of her feet out where Kevin could see it. "Let her hold your cock and jerk on it a little and then point it straight at my feet and push and let go. I bet you can do it."

"Really?" said Kevin. He held his dick for Sylvie to aim it.

"Of course!" said Marian.

"Okay," he said. Sylvie gripped the base of his cock and Kevin's stomach muscles tightened and he pressed his lips together and forced out a curve of hot piss that momentarily reached Marian's foot.

"That's the way!" said Marian. "How did it feel?"

"Felt good," said Kevin. "Kind of burny." He wiped the tip of his dick with his palm.

"Of course it did," Marian said. "Now, Sylvie? You know how badly you need to let it go. You know what's up my ass. How could you possibly be shy?" Again she tapped the flowers against Sylvie's cunt. "Push and piss it out for me."

Sylvie gave it a second try. She pushed very hard. After a moment, her tiny urethra opened and a clear spurt flared out. The flow stopped almost immediately.

"Good!" said Marian. "More!"

"But," Sylvie objected, "I'm pushing so hard I'm afraid something else might happen." She stood up. "I really *need* to use the bathroom—I'm not kidding."

"Oh, but I want to see that, too," said Marian. "I want to see everything you can do."

"Gross, no way!" said Sylvie.

Kevin decided that it was time for him to intercede. "I really don't think she can do that," he said. "I mean, I wouldn't mind at all if she did, but . . ."

Marian pulled off her dress in a quick motion. "Look at this dick up my ass." She leaned back on her hands and lifted her knees back against her body. "See that butthole? See how nice and tight it is? Look at that tight skin. You can look for as long as you want. Look at me rock on it. Can you see it moving in and out? Foo, that's nice! I like to see your eyes on it." She looked at them both and shook her tits for them. "Now, Sylvie, it's your turn. I've showed you, now you show me. Show me that tight little butt of yours again. See, I had no idea you were as full as I am. I want to see that ass open right up, just like mine is. Suck that cock of his and push it out for me. Once you do that, you'll feel free to do anything that feels good, anything you want, and you'll come extra hard, and that's what I want—I want you to come extra hard, because you can be damn sure that's what I'm going to do."

"I really have to go," said Sylvie. "I'm not kidding."

"I know you do! Squat down just like you were and suck that cock. I'll spray you clean, don't worry. Pull up on your cheeks so I can see. Push and let it go."

Sylvie took up her cocksucking squat. She started sucking more Kevin-dick, but faster than before. She pulled one of her cheeks open. Her asshole looked exactly the same—tiny, sexy. Then suddenly her piss gushed out everywhere.

"Ah, that's it!" said Marian, frigging her clit. "Show me how you let it all go. Release it. That's it. Let it all go. Feel it relax." Marian whisked the linen napkin out from under her toys and held it at the ready. "Let that lovely butt open right up for me."

Sylvie made a moan of warning. Her asshole domed out into a doughnut shape and began to open.

"Good!" said Marian. "Now stop! Tighten back up on it."

Sylvie made a straining sound. Her hips rocked, and her asshole slowly closed.

Marian was frigging faster now. She let the spray drive into Sylvie's ass. "That's right, honey," she coached. "Keep sucking that dick. I know you need to let it out. Push on it."

"It's really going to come out this time," said Sylvie, somewhat frantically. "I can't hold it."

"I know you can't hold it. I just want to see your ass open one more time. It's *so* sexy to see it open up. Let it go. Push now. Give it to us. Come on, push."

Sylvie moaned again. Her asshole domed and opened wider, and a big dark hard dickshape began to push its way straight out. Marian held the napkin underneath. "Oh yeah. Keep pushing, baby. Push it all out." She felt the weight drop in her hand and immediately folded the napkin over it and sprayed Sylvie clean. "*Now* we're ready!" she said. "We're ready to fuck, kids. Come on, Sylvie, get on your hands and knees over me. Open that cunt for Kevin's cock. I want to see Kevin's hard dick up your cunt while I pinch your nipples. Come on. I want to see some good hard fucking!"

But Sylvie didn't obey immediately. She had rights now. She was free to do anything she wanted. Boldly she lifted one of Marian's juggy tits and bent to slap it around with her tongue. Then, bringing her blond cunt-site close, she brushed Marian's nipple-tip over her neglected clit. "Could you hold those tits tight and point them right at my pussy?" she requested, with the zeal of a convert. "I think I've got a little pee left over for them." Sylvie pushed and let a brief spurt spray over Marian's mildly surprised breasts. "Let me hose it off," she said, and she took the showerhead from Marian and sprayed her mentor off.

"See?" said Marian, recovering quickly. "You can do anything now."

"Yeah, and *now* I'm ready for some cock. I need to be fucked good, Kev. Give it to me good."

She arranged herself on her elbows and knees over Marian's legs. Marian grabbed the girl's asscheeks and spread her open. Kevin got behind Sylvie; he stared at his girlfriend's impish twat as if he'd never seen it before and pumped his dick in his fast fist. It was a handsome dick, no question; watching him, Marian felt she needed to hold that purple stanchion for herself at least once. "Sylvie?" she asked. "You won't mind if I make sure your lover is good and stiff for you, will you?"

"No, just do it fast and get him in there!" said Sylvie, kissing her own bicep muscle. "Either that or shove one of those big dildo-dicks up my cunt and jerk him off onto my asshole. Your choice. But get something big up my cunt now!"

"I'll get him nice and fat for your cunt," said Marian. She surrounded Kevin's cock with her right hand and registered its warmth and livingly resisted rigidity. It felt, she found herself observing, extremely realistic. She steered its head toward the opening of Sylvie's pink slot and jerked its stem fairly hard in place a few times. "Feel the big head?" she said. "Wiggle a little for him. He's almost ready." She looked up at Kevin and mimed a licking mouth to show him how she would lick his dick if given the opportunity. He was aroused and slit-eyed, and, she noticed, he was gazing fixedly at her breasts.

"Could you please put him in now?" urged Sylvie.

"He's going to push it in now," Marian said, giving his dick a few last jerks. "Push that cock in her, baby." She held his shaft for as long as she could until it disappeared into Sylvie's cunt; Sylvie was very tight but equally wet, and the dick's length slid in without bending.

"Oh, fuck, that's good," said Sylvie, sighing with relief. Immediately she and Kevin started slapping fast against each other.

"Oh yeah! I like to see that dick slapping in there!" said Marian, turning the showerhead on her clit. "I can feel it in my cunt just looking at it! Yeah! My cunt is so empty and yours is so full of that sweet hot dickmeat!"

As they fucked, Sylvie focused on the dildos, which lay tumbled on the grass. The girl turned so that her face was close to Marian's. Her hair was in her eyes. In an uneven whisper, she said, "I need one of those. Pick one and put it in my ass, will you? Please?"

Marian brushed the tulips down Sylvie's back and tapped them against her asshole. Then she replaced the flowers with her middle finger, resting it lightly on the opening. "Is that where you want something? Right in there?"

"Oh," moaned Sylvie, "I want what's in your ass."

"Honey, I've got something much better than that for you," said Marian. "Kevin, look where my finger is. Isn't that a pretty little asshole? Has your cock ever been in there?"

Kevin shook his head no. His hands were on Sylvie's hips, and he was pushing with a circling motion of his hips, making gravelly grunts.

"I want to see that dick up that gorgeous little butt. That okay with you, Sylvie? You want your honey's big burning dick up your ass? Believe me, it'll feel good. You know you want it, don't you."

"Yeah I want it, I want it," said Sylvie.

"You want it straight up your ass, don't you," Marian repeated.

"I *need* it up my ass," Sylvie pleaded. "Kev, I need it up my ass!"

Marian grabbed the four-foot-long Welsh Fusilier and turned it on. She whispered to Sylvie, "Slide this up my cunt." Sylvie fumblingly obliged. "That's good. I want our slutty cunts to be connected while you get fucked up the ass for the first time," Marian said. She handed her end of it to Kevin. "Pull out of her, baby. Push this in instead." Kevin's long glossy dick emerged from behind the horizon of Sylvie's ass-curve and with evident reluctance he fed the end of the double-vibe where he had just been. Sylvie made a surprised shout and arched her back and started fucking against it.

As soon as Marian saw Kevin's cock reappear, she knew she had to suck it. This was her one chance. "Oh, God, that's a pretty cock," she said. "I need a real dick in my mouth for a second, just for a *second*. Come over here for a second, baby. Sylvie, he needs to be super stiff for your tight little butt. You don't mind if I get his dick good and stiff for you with my tongue, do you? I'm sorry, but I just have to suck on this dick."

"Suck him!" said Sylvie. "Ooh, God, suck him stiff for me. Just hurry and get something big up my ass. I'm so hot for it." She circled Marian's clit with her end of the Fusilier, gazing at the base of the Klockhammer buried in the older woman's ass. Marian, her mouth stuffed with purple cock, groaned and opened her legs for the pleasure. As Sylvie felt Kevin jabbing the other Welsh-head in and out of her own buzzing cunt-lips, she reached back and spread her asscheeks open and said, "That's enough. Stop sucking my boyfriend's dick and get it in my ass!"

Marian pulled her mouth off of Kevin's dick. "Okay, sweetie, it's ready for you." She squirted lube on Sylvie's asshole. The squirt bottle made rude noises, but nobody cared. She pulled Kevin into position by his cock and tapped the head of his dick on Sylvie's now-sloppy ass-crack, circling it over the opening. Then she pointed it and held it still. "Okay, push in slow, Kevin. Open up for him, Sylvie. He's going in."

"Push it in me! Fuck this ass!" cried Sylvie.

Marian held Kevin's cockshaft while it began to drive slowly in. It bent a little as he put his weight behind it; then, as Sylvie relaxed for him, it straightened out and filled her.

"There he goes," said Marian.

"Fuck me with that dick, oooooooo!" said Sylvie. Kevin began making very slow long strokes.

"That's it, Kevin—fuck straight into her perfect ass—you're getting it." Marian took hold of the end of the vibrator in her cunt and started pulling it in and out in rhythm with Kevin's steady dick-thrusts. Its length curved up and disappeared into Sylvie's clim. She kissed Sylvie on the shoulder. "God, I like being connected to your sexy pussy, sweetie!" she said. Sylvie was looking straight ahead, taking little breaths as she pushed back on Kevin's thickness. "You like him in your ass, don't you?" Marian asked her.

"I like him to fuck me hard!" said Sylvie. "Fuck my hot ass, Kev. I'm getting closer to the smiley face!" She looked at Marian. "That's what we say when we're going to come soon," she breathlessly explained.

Marian sprang into action. "Hold on, though—one last thing." She picked up the little okra-sized dildo and slipped it over her middle finger and squirted some Astroglide on it. "Can I put this in Kevin's ass?" she whispered. "I want to feel him fucking you when you come. Can I?"

Sylvie blew up on her bangs and nodded. "Just hurry." Marian flicked the okra-dick over Sylvie's nipples and then dragged it down Kevin's ribs and slid around to the base of his back and gripped the near cheek of his ass, so that her four fingers were near his asshole.

"What are you doing?" Kevin said, freezing suddenly.

"I'm putting some okra up your ass so you won't feel left out," said Marian. "I want to help you fuck Sylvie. I want to feel you fucking her ass, and I want your asshole to feel you fucking *her* asshole. Don't trouble yourself—just let it in and keep fucking."

"Let her do it, Kev!" Sylvie called earnestly.

Kevin overcame his uncertainty and resumed his slow, deliberate ass-fucking. But now, each time he pulled out for the next thrust, Marian drove the okra-dick a little farther into his reluctant male hole. He seemed to like it more after a minute or two, and as he began to get his own butt in gear, Marian started urging and guiding his movements, making him go a little faster, getting him to angle his thrusts, the way she knew Sylvie wanted it. Every push he made made his high-jumper's maximums-muscles bunch memorably under Marian's cupping hand. "See how she likes it faster?" Marian said. "Fuck her like this." She controlled his pumping torso with the okra-plug like a puppet-master and he said, "Oh, jeepers! Get it up there!"

"Pinch my nipples hard!" Sylvie ordered Marian in an urgent whisper. "I'm right *at* the smiley face," she called to Kevin.

"Let's get off together," said Marian, pinching as she was told. "Come on. Come on, come on. Fuck her, Kevin! Shoot that come in her. Look at this cock up my butt, Sylvie. Come over me. Oh! Oh fuck!" She let go of Sylvie's nipples and held the Welsh-head tight to her love-bean as her orgasm gathered the necessary signatures. The autographed Armande had been in her ass for so long that she felt the biggest climax of her life had to be well on its way. But she wasn't quite ready for it. She pushed her breasts forward and said, "Suck my tit-bags for a second, Sylvie. Suck them hard, bite them, bite them. Oh shit! Now come for me. Come around that hot dickmeat."

"Oh, God!" said Sylvie. She tried to suck Marian's nipples but couldn't concentrate on them and arched her neck, staring forward at the invisible pleasure in her head.

"That's okay—come for me, baby. She's starting to come, Kevin! Shoot that hot juice up her ass for her! Fill her ass with that burning come!" Marian finger-fucked the okra-dick faster in and out of Kevin's asshole, and he leaned forward to take it and then straightened up, lifting Sylvie by the hips right off the ground and pulling her back against his cock. "Now, Sylvie?" he said.

"Oh, fuck me good, Kev! Fill my fucking fanny!" Sylvie shouted, looking in Marian's eyes and then down at her toy-filled fuckholes. "Harder! Oh yes! Fuck me real good, darling! SHOOT THAT HOT DICK UP MY FANNY-HOLE! OH! OH!"

With an astonished expression, Kevin made one last long lurching shuddering push and started to come.

"OH YES!" said Sylvie, feeling Kevin's cock empty ounce after ounce of boiling scream-cream into her ass. "AH! I'M COMIIINNNG!!!!!" As pagan pleasures wracked her body, she did indeed make a huge grimacing smiley face.

It was Marian's turn now. She allowed the idea of Kevin's squirting dick in Sylvie's ass to merge with the sensation of Armande Klockhammer, Jr.'s in her own. She conjured up the sight of the dollar bills stuffed in his asscheeks as he danced with his back to the audience. She thought of the shouting women; the whomping music; the sight of him turning on the stage and tossing his heavy live meat around inside its black silk pouch as he looked out at all his women. All these memories were *up her ass*. She opened her eyes and said evenly, "Please watch me come, now, you two. Watch my asshole and cunt come around these huge horny cocks!" Then she threw herself back on the wet grass and lifted her legs and rested her feet on Sylvie's back; she let them watch whatever they wanted while the brutish, hunky orgasm ennobled her body. "Oh nice . . . so nice . . . so nice . . ." she sighed as the clit-twitching ebbed.

When the three of them had recovered a little, Marian rinsed off Kevin's softening cock and lifted herself off the Klockhammer and sprayed it fresh.

"Can we pick some more of your tulips sometime?" said Sylvie sweetly before she and Kevin, dressed once again in their matching outfits, left for the fish hatchery.

"Anytime you want," said Marian. "I love young love." Naked, replete, she put her toys and her abandoned book on the tray and went indoors. Over the next year, with Kevin and Sylvie's weekend help weeding and planting and mowing, her backyard became the envy of her neighbors.

(ONTRIBUTORS

Nicholson Baker's novels are *The Mezzanine, Room Temperature, Vox,* and *The Fermata.* He is also the author of an autobiographical work, *U and I.* His newest collection of essays is entitled *The Size of Thoughts* (1995).

Robert Olen Butler has published eight critically acclaimed books since 1981, including a volume of short fiction, *A Good Scent from a Strange Mountain,* which won the 1993 Pulitzer Prize for Fiction and which he has written into a screenplay for Ixtlan, Oliver Stone's production company. His stories have appeared widely in such publications as *Harper's, The Hudson Review,* and *The Sewanee Review,* and have been chosen for inclusion in three of the last four annual editions of *The Best American Short Stories.* He lives in Lake Charles, Louisiana, with his wife, the novelist and playwright Elizabeth Dewberry.

Tom Caffrey is the author of the collections *Hitting Home & Other Stories* and *Tales from the Men's Room.* His stories appear regularly in magazines including *Advocate Men, Honcho, Pucker Up, Torso,* and *Freshmen,* and are featured in the anthologies *Flesh and the Word 3* and *Ritual Sex.* He lives in New York City.

Renee M. Charles has published fiction in the horror, erotica, science fiction, fantasy, and western genres (under both her real name and this pen name) in over forty-five magazines and anthologies, including *The Industry*, from Circlet Press. She is also a fiction correspondence school instructor currently living in the Midwest.

Corwin Ericson is a poet and writer from Massachusetts. He is also the Senior Editor of *Paramour*, a quarterly magazine of literary and artistic erotica.

Scarlett Fever is a frequent contributor to *BUST*, where "Dating for Dollars" first appeared. No longer in the sex industry, she is working on a memoir of the nine years she spent there.

Le Shaun is currently pursuing her career as a rapper/stylist in the music industry. She has two singles on Tommy Boy, "Ready or Not" (1993) and "Wide Open" (1994).

Tsaurah Litzky lives in an apartment in Brooklyn with a view of the Statue of Liberty. Her work has appeared in *Ikon* and *Longshot* and will be included in the forthcoming *The Unbearables* anthology (Semiotext(e)/Autonomedia). Her two poetry chapbooks are *Pushing Out the Envelope* and *The Blue Bird Buddha of No Regrets* (Apathy Press, Baltimore, 1992, 1994). She writes an "Eros and Existence" page for the New York-based paper *Downtown*.

Al Lujan is an East Los Angeles *joto* (queer) living in San Francisco; a poet, visual and performance artist. He is a member of Piel de Dios, a Latino gay men's writing group. He is an aide at Coming Home Hospice. He has performed his own work at Llego's festival of Latino Gay & Lesbian performance and at the AIDS Theatre Festival.

Mary Malmros is (in no particular order) a writer, Internet denizen, martial artist, and paid networking lackey. She lives in interesting times in Boston, where she works on inventing a thirty-six-hour day and gives thanks daily for having too many good times to fit in the standard twenty-four-hour variety.

Jay Michaelson is a pen name of Erich Michael Thomas, a creative SubGenius. "The Spirit that Denies" is an excerpt from a work in progress. He and a handful of others continue to carry on the "good work" at the Thought Shop outside of Washington, D.C.

Susan Musgrave is a poet, novelist, and columnist who lives on Vancouver Island, Canada. Her latest book of poetry, *Forcing the Narcissus,* was published by McClelland and Stewart in the spring of 1994. A second book of personal essays, *Musgrave Landing: Musings on the Writing Life* was published by Stoddart, also in the spring. "Valentine's Day in Jail" is excerpted from a novel in progress, *Cover Girl.* She is Writer in Residence at the University of Toronto for 1995.

Anna Nymus is a pseudonym for a journalist who has spent many years in different European countries, where she has been actively engaged in the women's movement. She has published erotic short stories in several European women's magazines under this pen name. She is working on an erotic novel in Berkeley, California.

Lisa Palac is the producer of the erotic virtual audio series "Cyborgasm." Former host of the talk radio show "Generation Sex," she is currently working on a book about her adventures in pop sex culture. She is the founding editor of *Future Sex* magazine. Her work has appeared in *Details, The Village Voice, The London Observer, Playboy, Penthouse,* the erotica anthologies *Herotica I* and *II,* and *Best American Erotica 1993.* She lives in San Francisco.

Paul Reed is the author of thirteen books, including the novels *Facing It* and *Longing* and the nonfiction journals *The Savage Garden* and *The Q Journal*. Writing as Max Exander, he has authored five volumes of erotica. He lives in San Francisco.

Annie Regrets, a.k.a. Margaret Weigel, is a Boston-based writer, musician, and designer whose mother is still blissfully unaware that her daughter is no longer a virgin.

Susan St. Aubin began writing erotica in 1984 and hasn't been able to stop. Her stories have been anthologized in all three volumes of *Herotica, Yellow Silk: Erotic Arts and Letters, Erotic By Nature,* and *Fever: Sensual Stories by Woman Writers.*

Raye Sharpe is an East Coast writer whose work has appeared in *Paramour* magazine. She began writing to stimulate the imaginations of those who complain about the limitations of safe sex, and is currently working on a collection of her short stories. She dedicates "30" to Amelia, her bold soul sister.

Trac Vu grew up in Saigon, Paris, and San Francisco. He graduated from UC Berkeley with a B.A. in English in 1991 and currently lives in Los Angeles, where he is pursuing a career in film production.

Anne Wallace is a mother, educator, writer, and adventurer from Long Beach, California. She has published fiction and articles in journals as diverse as *13th Moon* and *Redbook.*

James Williams has published fiction and nonfiction in *Advocate Men, Spectator, Attitude,* and *Sandmutopia Guardian*. His story, "Trust," will appear in *SM Futures*, a 1995 anthology edited by Cecilia Tan for Circlet Press, and in a subsequent anthology from Richard Kasak Books. He lives in San Francisco.

READER'S DIRECTORY

Manic D Press

Publisher of underground and subversive literature by emerging writers. Jennifer Joseph, Publisher/Editor. P.O. Box 410804, San Francisco, CA 94141. Complete catalog $1.00.

Black Sheets

Intelligent, irreverent, sex-positive magazine. Bill Brent, Editor. P.O. Box 31155-A95, San Francisco, CA 94131; 1-800-818-8823 for credit card orders. Subscriptions are $20/4 issues, payable to The Black Book, with a statement of legal age required; a sample issue is $6.50 postpaid. A free publications catalog is also available.

Paramour Magazine

Literary and artistic erotica. Amelia Copeland, Publisher/Editor. P.O. Box 949, Cambridge, MA 02140. Published quarterly; subscriptions are $18/year; samples are $4.95.

Masquerade Books

World's leading publisher of straight, gay, lesbian, and S/M erotic literature. Richard Kasak, Publisher. 801 Second Avenue, New York, NY 10017. Bi-monthly *Masquerade Erotic Newsletter* subscriptions are $30/year; book catalogs are free.

Conjunctions

Bi-annual volumes of new writing. Bradford Morrow, Editor. Bard College, Annandale-on-Hudson, NY 12504. Published bi-annually; subscriptions are $18/year.

BUST

The magazine that's strong enough for a man, but made for a woman. Marcelle Karp & Debbie Stoller, Editors/Publishers. P.O. Box 319, Ansonia Station, New York, NY 10023. Published quarterly; subscriptions are $10/year.

Circlet Press

A small independent book publisher specializing in erotic science fiction and fantasy. Cecilia Tan, Editor/Publisher. P.O. Box 15143, Boston, MA 02215. Send SASE for catalog.

Pink Pages
Beet

Just like literary quarterlies, but interesting. Joe Maynard, Publisher. 372 5th Avenue, Brooklyn, NY 11215. Three copies are $7, single copies are $2.

Venus Infers

This leatherdyke quarterly ceased publication in early 1995; however, back issues full of high-quality fiction, photography, and articles are still available. Pat Califia, Publisher, 2215R Market Street, Box 261, San Francisco, CA 94114. Send SASE for more information.

CREDITS

READER SURVEY

What are your favorite stories in this year's collection?

Have you read previous years' editions of Best American Erotica? (1993 or 1994)

If yes, do you have any favorite stories from those previous collections?

Do you have any recommendations for next year's Best American Erotica? (Any nomination must be a story that was published in the United States, in any form, during the 1995 calendar year).

How did you purchase this book?

____independent bookstore   ____chain bookstore
____mail order company   ____other type of store
____sex/erotica shop   ____borrowed it from a
    friend

What made you interested in BAE 1995:

____enjoyed other *BAE* collections   ____editor's reputation
____authors' reputations   ____enjoy "Best Of" type
____word-of-mouth   anthologies in general
  recommendation   ____read book review

Any other suggestions? Feedback?
Please return this survey or any other *BAE*-related correspondence to: Susie Bright, *BAE* Feedback, 3311 Mission St., #143, San Francisco, CA 94110, or you can e-mail me at: BAEfeedbk@aol.com

Thanks so much.